THE ORPHAN'S JOURNEY

Elizabeth's Beginning

Camille Jeffers

Interior and Cover design by Trinity Hills Publishing
Publisher affirms that author holds all rights of final approval of the content of this book. Publisher rights to editorial changes including spelling, punctuation and grammar are subject to approval of the author.

Trinity Hills Publishing
Exposing great minds
92 Cipero Road
Retrench Village
San Fernando
Trinidad and Tobago
www.trinityhillspublishing.com

Table of Contents

C h a p t e r   O n e

✻ ✻ ✻

The Orphanage

Orphanage. The idea of this very word may give one the feeling of an almost dilapidated, musty building, crammed with a battalion of noisy, dirty, ill-behaved, ill-mannered, ill-treated, and underfed children, at the mercy of nonchalant and disenchanted or warden-like guardians, as they wait to be adopted into loving families. This orphanage that you have begun to read about is not at all like that! In fact, it was no ordinary orphanage at all.

Here, newborn babies shared a nursery, while toddlers from the ages of one to four years old were kept in other quarters.

Each nursery was equipped with its' own caregiver and a volunteer assistant. Children from the ages of five to seven years old were kept in groups of five per bedroom, also with their own caregivers – one to each bedroom. Children from ages eight to twelve years old were kept in groups of three per bedroom, again, with a caregiver and volunteer assistant assigned to each bedroom.

Teenagers from the age of thirteen to eighteen however, were arranged for differently as their social, psychological, and physical development required a different approach. Every adolescent at the age of thirteen was given their own room, which remained theirs until they reached the age of eighteen. They were required to submit to weekly check-ins by the Dean of the orphanage, and daily check-ins by a specifically assigned caregiver.

This system promoted the development of individuality and responsibility, as well as trust between all parties involved. Privacy and accountability were both given at the same time. Each child was given a sense of responsibility as they were charged with the jobs of keeping their quarters neat and clean at all times, assisting each other with tasks, and keeping their grades at a certain level. There was undoubtedly enough space, accommodation, and loving, professionally qualified caregivers for all the children present at the orphanage which at the time, amounted to one hundred and seventy children in total.

This orphanage was their haven, where children who had lost their parents or family members through different means such as violence, abandonment or unforeseen incidents, would have a place of their own to live, develop, and be positively guided and influenced. That is, until a family adopts them or they turn eighteen and go off to college, and by extension, the adult world. The orphanage was named The Phoenix Foundation, taking after one of the most interesting of mythical creatures called the Phoenix.

Just as a Phoenix dies and is reborn from its ashes, ready to take on the world once more, the same analogy can be applied to the orphaned. Once they begin their life at the orphanage and continue outside of it, through social interaction with others such as new family members, this becomes a new beginning for them, where they get a chance to take on the world and family life once more. The orphanage was equipped with a school, amongst other facilities.

Children were academically instructed from kindergarten

to high school where, nearing the end of high school, each student was required to fill out college applications as well as find a part-time job. They were guided and assisted accordingly with these two steps that played an important role in the next chapter of their lives. As was custom, the government assisted with college fees where necessary. However, some students received scholarships, while others acquired student loans to pursue their course of study.

There were various measures in place to ensure that each child would have a smooth transition into their own life stably and on their own two feet. This process of transition into the adult world had worked well over the past years, and continued to work well due to the implementation of various development and training programs, to assist the now young adults begin the new chapter of their lives. Each child in the orphanage was often enrolled in programs that encouraged them to contribute positively in some way to their community.

Equipped also with a Health Facility, Library, Recreational Area, and Counseling Center, even children who had experienced a very tumultuous or difficult past, were able to receive the help they needed from the counselors who were aptly qualified in the areas of Grief and Guidance Counseling.

Occasionally, the orphans were taken on field trips which were sometimes sponsored by other institutions, or by the inviting host.

Weekly religious instruction sessions also played an integral role in their program. They were given a strong spiritual foundation on which they were encouraged to build on through prayer, meditation, and volunteer work. Every month, the children contributed ideas on activities that they could work on together in order to give back to the community in the form of food-drives, clean-up drives, or fun-fairs.

Clearly, this was not a typical orphanage! Once a dream, it came to fruition by the original owner, Mr. Christopher Walters, who was the father of the current Dean and owner. He was one man that changed the world with his heart. It was his desire that the highest of priorities be placed on the needs and development of the children, and he worked very hard to maintain that focus. The directors of the Phoenix Foundation, who resided locally as well as internationally, shared the same vision and eagerly sponsored items for both the children and the orphanage itself.

They also implemented programs that partnered the orphanage with various institutions and firms, to help graduates receive entrepreneurial and on-the-job training opportunities, that focused on individuality, creativity, leadership, and team building. This orphanage created the ideal atmosphere and environment for children, youngsters, and teenagers, who were victims of varying degrees of trauma and negative circumstances, to be nurtured and developed into well rounded and ambitious citizens, contributing what they can to the world around them.

C h a p t e r   T w o

✳ ✳ ✳

The Beginning

As she slept in her bed that night, flashbacks of the accident tormented her mind. She tossed and turned, and with every turn there came a fresh assault of painful memories, drawing her back into the abyss of the event that changed her life forever. She remembered the rain - the look of it, the feel of it - like cold liquid diamonds falling from the eyes of angels. Even the smell of it was still so fresh in her mind's eye.

She remembered her parents covered in their own blood, being carried to the waiting ambulances, whose red lights roiled like silent alarms, signaling the true gravity of what had just happened. There was a blur of medics and policemen that seemed to be frantically running around everywhere, trying to make sense of the situation that had so suddenly descended upon them. The shouts and screams of bystanders and victims were so sharp and terrifying, that she too began to cry and sob uncontrollably.

As had become her custom at this point, she awoke abruptly from her sleep, sitting up, gasping for breath, teary-eyed, and completely soaked in sweat. "7:30 a.m." she muttered to herself as she glanced at her clock, regained control of her breathing, and slumped back onto her pillow. After a few seconds of gathering her thoughts, she began her morning ritual. She closed her eyes, thanked God for the new day despite her tumultuous night, and for the blessings to come in the day ahead.

She also prayed that today, maybe this very day, she would meet a family that wanted to adopt her, but this was something she kept her hopes low for, in order to cushion the blow of the chance that this may not happen. She then reached into the top drawer of her bedside table, and removed from it a hidden treasure. This item, though tattered and wrinkled from the experiences of kisses and tears in conjunction with the passage of time, was so near and dear to her, that just the knowledge of its presence brought a smile to her often lonely heart.

She closed her eyes and kissed the picture of her parents that was her very last good memory of them. It was one of - if not the most - prized of her possessions, which was why when she kissed that picture, she quickly wiped away the solitary tear that rolled down her cheek. She did this in order to protect the already fragile artefact in her hands. After five minutes of clutching the photograph to her chest as she lay in bed, she arose, placed the precious item back into the safety of the drawer, and proceeded to the bathroom to get ready for school.

Today was Friday and at the orphanage, school began promptly at 9:00 a.m. Elizabeth got dressed, grabbed her backpack, and hurried out of her room. She returned a few seconds later, and grabbed up a folder that was stuffed with pages that lay on her desk. She made her way down the hall, clutching the folder to her chest. She delighted in the quietness of her journey, and came to a halt when she arrived at her destination.

Here, she closed her eyes and smiling, she basked in the quiet comfort of the place that she had grown so fond of. Slowly, Elizabeth walked to the bench that overlooked the school's football field. This bench was her creative cocoon. With this bench she shared her most intimate of moments, pouring herself onto pages upon pages of captivating images and words. She sat on the bench and gazed appreciatively at the morning scenery.

She smiled to herself, as she felt such comfort emanating from the warm kisses of the sun dancing across her face. There was such a feeling of serenity that flowed through her mind, body, and seemingly her spirit, as she absorbed even the very image of the final drops of dew, escaping from the shrubs and lawn nearby. Elizabeth was a beautiful young lady both internally and externally. She was of average height and slim, with long, curly, black hair that she always wore in a bun.

Her caramel complexion and rosy lips complimented her well, as did the obvious dimples she possessed in each cheek that added to the innocence that her face held. Almost always, she would be seen in a T-shirt, jeans, hoodie, and her backpack of books that she carried EVERYWHERE. She spent her time getting lost in her books. So lost, that time usually slipped by without her noticing. Despite her intelligence and vast knowledge, she barely spoke and lacked confidence in this same knowledge.

Due to her socially awkward demeanour, she was hardly ever noticed and at times, she preferred it that way, as it gave her the ability to disappear and spend more time reading, drawing, and writing. Even though Elizabeth was not a very social person, she was not in the least bit bothered by it. She had enough friendship experience to know that she did not want the pain that came with having them. Friends that she held dear almost always seemed to be taken from her.

Some friends were adopted, which was a natural and regular part of orphanage life, while others either outgrew her or stopped talking to her altogether without explanation or cause. For this, she thought the reason was her lack of interest in what others liked at her age. They found her to be peculiar. The only person that had stuck with her this far for a reason beyond her comprehension, was Stephan. It puzzled her greatly when he started referring to her as his best friend, but it wasn't enough to change her view of friendships, despite him being her friend for eleven years.

He would always check up on her everyday, sometimes multiples times per day. He was also welcomed to be physically present while she wrote or drew, but not allowed to pry into this world of hers. He would also listen intently when she spoke about everything, and even be by her side when she cried about her broken friendships, or when the memory of her parents became overwhelming.

They met each other at the orphanage and had one thing in

common; the loss of both their parents. Stephan's parents were murdered by thieves, who broke into their house one stormy Saturday evening. His father was killed while trying to fight off the bandits to protect his wife and son. Stephan remembered the screams of his father telling his mother to run. He remembered watching his father scuffle with the two intruders, as he cried with outstretched arms to seemingly grab his father from the temporary safety of his mother's arms, while she ran upstairs with him.

His mother, fearing for the safety of her young child, gently told him that he had to be quiet, and that she would be right back. She then gently placed him in his toy chest, reminded him to be quiet, kissed his forehead, and gently closed the lid. He remembered how it felt when she kissed his forehead. He felt the tremble of her hands and lips. As he lay among his toys in the chest, he heard her footsteps run out of the room and seconds later, he heard a loud sound.

This was the same sound he heard when his father was fighting the bandits. The authorities found the small boy, four years old at the time, passed out in the toy chest. Both his parents were dead. He had no other family who was able to take him in at the time, so the Foundation accepted the responsibility when his story was brought to their attention. Stephan, now fifteen years old, was a lot more popular than his introverted best friend.

He was tall with a muscularly developed frame, and a vanilla complexion. He had a mess of short, jet- black, straight hair which he would always cut into a neat mohawk. His Japanese ancestry was quite evident from his facial features, and this striking young man maintained an excellent symmetry between a rigorous academic schedule, and an equally rigorous sports program. He participated in everything the orphanage had to offer!

Quite popular with the girls, Stephan showed little interest in relationships with anyone, except for the girl he had come to love so deeply over the years. All that he did for her and with her, was because of his love for her that he held so dear. A love he wanted to share with her alone but sadly, she only saw him as her best friend. So many years had passed and his feelings for her never waned. He hoped with all his heart that one day she would finally come to see his love, and confess that she felt the same for him.

He sometimes laughed to himself at the possibility of this happening, but he was always comforted in knowing that as long as they were still friends, hope for a future with her still existed. She was his one true friend and he was hers, and that for now, was more than enough.

C h a p t e r   T h r e e

✻✻✻

The Encounter

Elizabeth made herself comfortable on the bench and carefully, almost ceremoniously, opened the folder. This folder contained two compartments; one on either side. These compartments held the doorway to a beautiful hidden world, where her creative genius was unleashed, free to roam wild and untethered by time, limitations or the criticisms, expectations, and opinions of others. Here on these pages, she was free to express her feelings, ideas, and concepts in her own way.

In one compartment, she kept drawings and poems she had completed over the years. The other compartment contained blank sheets of paper for masterpieces yet to be created. Removing one of these blank sheets, she closed the folder and placed the page on the front of it. She retrieved a sharpened pencil from her backpack, briefly stared at the scenery laid before her and after a few seconds, Elizabeth began to sketch.

The young artist would often sketch everything around her; buildings, people both known and unknown to her, landscapes, and even the weather! From the most picturesque to the seemingly blandest of items, nothing escaped her eye or her pencil. It was certainly a true gift, one that she had come to cherish greatly, and was most thankful for. She was so focused on what she was doing, lost in her own creative trance, that she didn't realize that someone came to stand next to her, silently witnessing her astounding talent, and completely mesmerized by the degree of accuracy with which she expressed what she saw.

Time seemed to disappear so quickly until alas! Her focus was interrupted by the sudden scream of the school's bell. "Brrrrrriiiiiiiiiiiiiiiiinnnnnnnngggg!" She looked up sharply from her unfinished work, as her mind was jolted back to reality. She nodded and smiled at the view before her, as if to give thanks for the honour of sketching it. Suddenly, something caught her attention. Something?

No, someONE moved at the corner of her eye! As she spun sideways to catch a good look at who or what it was, her bottom jaw almost instantaneously hit her knee, as she came face to face with the Dean of the orphanage, Mrs. Samantha Hamilton. She was literally slightly bent over, fixated on the incomplete sketch that lay on Elizabeth's lap! Samantha was a tall and slender lady, with a very light complexion and dyed, shoulder length, straight, red hair.

She would always wear structured dresses, sometimes with an accompanying jacket and high heels. Her face was oval shaped with high cheek-bones, and beautiful grey eyes, which could be seen through the glasses she always wore. Her teeth were pearl white, and she had a very contagious smile which couldn't help but spread across her face in this moment. From ear to ear, she beamed at such talent that had been so carefully hidden all this time.

"What a treasure!" she thought to herself. Elizabeth however, began to stammer and stutter while her face flushed red. "I…. umm… err…ummmm…" and when she realized that her words had completely abandoned her, she hurriedly stuffed all her things into her backpack. Awash with embarrassment and as red as a beet, she managed to whisper, "I'm sorry," and quickly hopped off the bench and bolted past Mrs. Hamilton as fast as her human legs could carry her.

Mrs. Hamilton, now upright, remained speechless. The first reason for her lack of speech was because she had never in all her life witnessed with her own two eyes, so much raw talent embedded in such a young, shy, and awkward person. Secondly, her mind became alarmed by the look of sheer terror on the child's face, that she didn't really know what to say or do to take away the obvious embarrassment, and the discomfort of the situation.

Samantha had known Elizabeth for years so she knew that she was an introvert, very withdrawn, and not involved in a lot of activities, clubs or projects that the Foundation offered. This was why she was so shocked at her discovery that day. Looking at Elizabeth draw was like witnessing a masterpiece being created before her very eyes, and it was such a delightful surprise! "How could I know this child for so many years, and not know that this naturally creative side of her ever existed?" she asked herself incredulously.

Mrs. Hamilton let out a sigh of disappointment in herself, as she thought that maybe she could've handled the situation with a little more finesse, rather than gawking at the child's work in such an ill-mannered fashion. She then slowly made her way to the school's auditorium to conduct the morning's assembly, thinking deeply as she went.

C h a p t e r   F o u r

✳ ✳ ✳

Samantha's Assignment

As Elizabeth ran toward the assembly area, a plethora of questions bombarded her mind. "How long had Dean Hamilton been standing there? How much did she see? I wonder if she thinks I'm a weirdo? What if she tells everyone at school and they all laugh at me?" She froze at the thought of all the tutors, caregivers, and counselors sneering and laughing at her in the staff lounge. A chill ran down her spine at this thought.

She resumed movement, and though her running had now turned into walking, her mind kept racing. She couldn't help how she felt. No one had ever been allowed entry into her private world of art, not even Stephan! He would be present, but he

19

would respect her by giving her the space she usually asked for. He never peeked, no matter how tempting it was. She felt so open, vulnerable even, as she thought about the breach in her most secure space.

Her walking then slowed down to a crawl until she finally stopped completely. "Okay Lizzie," she thought to herself, "maybe it's not that bad." She took a deep breath and tried to settle her nerves, thinking that despite the trespass, maybe Dean Hamilton didn't see anything much. By the time she reached the assembly area, she had made up her mind that her best option was to pretend that nothing major had happened, and to not focus too much on it.

That day was undoubtedly the weirdest and longest school day in the history of school days ever. Dean Hamilton seemed to be popping up everywhere! Elizabeth thought that she was just being paranoid, but little did she know that she was not! Dean Hamilton really did shadow Elizabeth that entire day! She had become so intrigued by the little creature, and curious to know more about the everyday activity of this child that she apparently knew nothing about.

She felt compelled to know more about her capabilities and interests, so she resorted to observing her for the entire day.

When Samantha Hamilton got home that day, the first thing she did was call her mother. Samantha's father, Christopher Walters, died five years prior due to a massive heart attack. Since that incident, she had been sure to maintain a very close relationship with her mother. She checked in on her daily, and spoke to her about everything.

Apart from her husband, Samantha's mother Nadine, was her closest friend and most trusted confidant. Nadine preferred the comfort of her home and therefore turned down the invitation to live with Samantha and David after her husband died. Samantha felt uncomfortable with this arrangement. Not wanting to place her in the care of a Senior Citizen's Home as she progressed in age, Samantha hired a caregiver that lived with Mrs. Walters, accompanied her wherever she wanted to go, and helped her with her daily functions as needed.

This arrangement was better for all parties, as someone was present with her at all times in order to monitor her, help her, and keep her company. As she spoke, her mother listened intently - not only to what her daughter was saying, but also to the discomfort in her voice. Samantha usually gave her mother a full report of the day's happenings, however, today there was something different in the way she spoke.

When she got tired of waiting for her daughter to tell her what the problem was, she gently said, "Sam, there is something weighing heavily on your heart and mind. So much so, that I can hear the weight of it in your voice. What is it honey?" Shocked by her mother's question, Samantha remained quiet for all of ten seconds, let out a loud sigh, then started pouring her heart out to her mother about Elizabeth, the day's findings about this girl, and the inexplicable yet compelling tug on her heart for her.

She knew that she didn't feel the way she did just out of pity for her circumstance nor her talent. It was immensely more than just that. She felt such a connection with Elizabeth that was in itself all the more confusing, because she had no idea why. "Well, maybe she is your assignment honey," her mother replied with an unmistakable smile in her voice. "My assignment?" Samantha responded quizzically. "What does that even mean?" she asked, as she shifted uncomfortably on the sofa.

Her mother began to explain saying, "Sam, every person on this planet has been placed here with an assignment. Each assignment may be different, but they all have one goal in common and that is to help. It seems like you found your assignment today. This girl, from what you have told me, has lost everyone yet she finds ways to hold on to the one thing that brings some joy to her, despite what she has gone through."

"She has been blessed with such talent and artistic insight so that she can express herself, and find the happiness to soothe her soul. I'm sure she feels like her art is an extension of herself; her defining characteristic, a cherished and well-protected element, reserved only for herself and God. An element that she uses as her very own cocoon, where she can be free and feel safe. She may have felt embarrassed today because you intruded into a space that she has never given anyone access to."

"You took a peek and saw her in her most uninhibited moment, and THAT is why she got scared. She now feels like her security – her safe place – has been compromised, hence her reaction." "Oh my," Samantha said, now with a better grasp of the young teen's disposition. "I didn't think about it like that mom." Chuckling, she continued saying, "Elizabeth has been at the orphanage for eleven years, and I am clueless about her."

"You have only heard about her for eleven minutes and somehow you seem to understand her and her situation infinitely better than I do." Nadine chuckled back at her daughter and said, "It's either a gift or years of experience. Either way, I'm usually right." In a more serious tone, she continued, "Now listen dear, I think that God has sent this child to you. You are each other's assignment, and you will teach her just as much as she will teach you."

"Be careful though. You must tread lightly, because if you come on too strong, she will clam up and shut you out completely. Let her warm up to you." "I understand mom, but I don't know if I am ready for all of this. I have not gotten over the loss of Anastasia. I still miss her soooooo much," responded Samantha with a deep sense of concern in her voice. "That's perfectly fine dear, and no one will ever take Ana's place."

"It's okay to think that you are not ready, however, the tug that you feel in your heart toward this child reveals something different. I believe that God has sent her into your life, and your spirit accepts that. He who has begun a good work, is faithful to complete it to the very end," Nadine said consolingly, as a single tear rolled down Samantha's cheek without her even realizing. The sound of Mr. Hamilton's vehicle pulling into the garage interrupted the conversation.

As she tried to regain her composure, she said, "Thanks mom. I think David just got home, so I'll talk to you tomorrow. Take care and I love you ok?" "I love you too honey," Nadine responded lovingly. "Oh and Sam, let me know how everything goes with Elizabeth," she added quickly. After Samantha assured her that she would tell her everything, Nadine then hung up. Samantha Hamilton, or "Sam" as those closest to her fondly called her, leaned forward on the sofa, allowing herself a brief moment to silently process all that her wise mother had told her over the phone.

Chapter   Five

✳✳✳

A Muddle of Thoughts

"Why would God, knowing what happened to us, send a child as an assignment?" Sam thought silently, most bewildered at the idea. With a deep breath and a loud sigh, she leaned back into the comfort of the sofa. Closing her eyes, Samantha raised her face toward the ceiling, and asked God to help and guide her, and to give her the wisdom to deal with the situation properly, as she knew that the coming days would indeed be crucial.

David, upon entering the room, saw his wife sitting on the sofa with her eyes closed. Sauntering toward her, he greeted her with a gentle kiss on her cheek. David was originally of Australian descent. He was taller than Samantha, but medium built. He had a caramel complexion, and was muscular, but not overly so. He had dark brown, curly hair, which he usually kept in a low fade, and a short beard and mustache neatly decorated his round face.

Both he and Sam were forty-four years old, but one could never tell by looking at them. Their expression of love for each other was like that of a newly married couple, despite being married for nineteen years. Mustering a smile, Sam sat up on the sofa and opened her eyes. Studying his wife's face however, he could tell that something was on her mind. Though she tried to conceal it by asking him about his day and what he would like to have for dinner, David knew his wife all too well.

"What's on your mind love?" he asked gently as he sat on the sofa and removed his shoes. "Hmmm….," she said with little sigh and a slight frown, as he put his arm around her. Samantha lay her head on her husband's shoulder and told him everything that happened that day – from her encounter with Elizabeth, to her phone conversation with her mother. "Well Sam, maybe she IS your assignment. Or maybe, you feel so drawn to this girl because of our Anastasia."

"Remember after Ana died, you said that you felt a desire to be there for kids who had lost their parents, just like this girl you are talking about? Is it that she reminds you of Ana?" As David asked these questions, Samantha pondered on them very carefully. Not only on the questions, but also on the response that she would give. Uncontrollably though, as she processed her husband's questions, tears began to trickle down her face.

Seeing her reaction, David embraced his wife and apologized for bringing up the loss of their daughter. Anastasia Hamilton was eight years old when her life was stolen in a vehicular accident. That day was indeed the most tragic and saddest day in the otherwise blissful lives, of David and Samantha Hamilton. It was also the most difficult to forget. From what they could recall, it was raining heavily that day.

A couple who had lost control of their brakes, was hit by a truck, skidded on the wet road, and collided with a light pole. The impact of the collision threw their vehicle into the oncoming traffic on the opposite side of the highway. The first vehicle that they crashed into was that of the Hamilton's. Their daughter was seated in the back seat on the right side, in the direct pathway of the tumbling car. She was killed instantly.

It had been a difficult process, and a very long healing road for both David and Samantha. That wound, however, was still tender to the touch. Even though eleven years had already passed since the accident, bittersweet thoughts and fond memories of their beautiful daughter, were very much present and alive in both their hearts and minds. Samantha Hamilton however, was not the only one deep in thought at that moment.

Young Elizabeth sat at the head of her bed, wedged in the corner of the wall, hugging her knees, and staring at the wall on the opposite side of the room. The pretty yellow sunflowers on the wallpaper seemed to blur, as her mind lost itself in a muddle of thoughts. She ran a gamut of emotions, as she dissected the day's experiences all over again; embarrassed, afraid, vulnerable, embarrassed some more, and finally, very awkward because now, she would be seeking to avoid Dean Hamilton at any cost.

Suddenly, a random surge of confidence disturbed her depressed mood. "You know what Lizzie?" she said aloud to herself. "These things happen. That's life! How much could she really have seen? And besides, that's MY spot! No one has ever claimed it, and I've never seen her or anyone else there before. That's why I chose it in the first place, so why should I stop going?! This was just a weird, freaky, one-time thing, and I'm freaking out for no reason!"

"She may have already forgotten about me and what she

may, or may not, have seen anyway. Tomorrow is a new day, and life goes on. Besides, who cares about a geeky fourteen-year-old anyway?" Elizabeth didn't even realize that she had gotten off her bed, and had begun pacing as she spoke. With that, Elizabeth resolved in herself that she was overreacting, and the next time she wanted to sketch, she would be going back to her sacred spot.

She closed her eyes and smiled to herself, as she reminisced about how peaceful and beautifully quiet it was there. It was as though God Himself had chosen that place for her, where she felt so safe and free to express herself. There was no way that she was staying away from her spot! "Dean Hamilton will have to find another one because that one is already taken!" She mused to herself. With fresh resolve and adrenaline, Elizabeth went off to shower and pray.

She then settled at her desk to do her homework. When she was done, she began to review the morning's, now completed, masterpiece. A few minutes later, the tired teen fell asleep. A knock on her door the next morning, shook Elizabeth out of her sleep. She glanced at the clock. "8:17 a.m." she muttered. It was Saturday. People rarely visited her, and check-ins were not scheduled for another forty-three minutes.

So she lay in bed, about to drift back off to sleep for a few more minutes, thinking that maybe someone knocked on her door by mistake. That thought was quickly dismissed by a second knock. She groggily got out of bed and drifted to the door. "Who is it?" she asked in a small voice. No answer. She repeated the question, this time, a little louder but still, no response. She opened the door, just enough to get a peek at who was on the other side.

Her eyes widened with disbelief, and all effects of slumber seemed to immediately vanish from her body, as she beheld Samantha Hamilton standing outside her door, with a small box in her hand.

C h a p t e r   S i x

❋ ❋ ❋

Clarity

"Ummm…I'm sorry Elizabeth," Mrs. Hamilton said nervously, "I didn't respond because I … err…... wanted to surprise you so ummm…. surprise!" she continued, just as nervously as she had begun. The reality however, was that Samantha had temporarily forgotten her own name and her reason for showing up! Elizabeth opened the door fully and shyly said, "It's no problem Dean Hamilton."

"You can come in, and please excuse the mess." Samantha gingerly entered the room, and after glancing around, immediately adopted a most confused expression on her face. She had never seen such a well-kept and organized room belonging to a teenager before. After intently scanning the room for the "mess", she finally asked Elizabeth, "What mess?" her confusion quite obvious by her tone. Sheepishly, Elizabeth responded, "Last night I fell asleep at my desk, and I crawled into bed around 3:00 a.m. without putting these items away."

Hurriedly, she packed her books and materials away. Though she was fourteen years old, Elizabeth was as shy as a baby deer. Doing her best not to add to the potential awkwardness of the moment, Mrs. Hamilton said, "I brought your breakfast," smiling awkwardly as she gave the little box to Elizabeth. Noticing the strange smile, Elizabeth thanked her politely, and then asked quite sarcastically, "Is room service on a Saturday a new thing at the orphanage?"

Samantha's cheeks turned bright red with embarrassment. "Ummm …. no," she responded, "in fact, I wanted to speak to you about yesterday." Elizabeth's heart began to beat so fast and so loudly, that it seemed to drown out everything else in the room. The tiny hairs on the back of her neck stood needle straight, and her blood seemed to run cold, as she mentally replayed the previous day's debacle.

She motioned for Mrs. Hamilton to have a seat at her now clean desk, while she sat at the edge of her bed, awaiting the words to come. "First off, please allow me to apologize for what happened," began Mrs. Hamilton. "You see, I had a lot on my mind yesterday, so to relax myself, I needed to go for a walk. I find calm in nature and just by being alone sometimes. Because I was at work, I decided to go to the field where I knew that seeing the sunlight glistening on the bright green, grassy field, and the beautiful blue sky with soft, fluffy clouds, would have made me feel so much better," she continued animatedly.

"Imagine my surprise when I arrived and saw that someone was already there so early in the morning, and a student no less! What piqued my curiosity even more, was that you seemed so engrossed in what you were doing, that you didn't even hear or notice when I came up behind you to see what was taking place. When I got close enough, I looked over your shoulder to peek at what had gripped your attention so completely."

"I was literally awestruck at the level of skill that I was witnessing firsthand! The passion that I saw on your face, was a perfect match with every stroke of your pencil. I was so captivated by all this, that I didn't think I was trespassing into your world. I snapped back to reality when the bell rang, and it was in that moment when I saw the look of sheer horror and embarrassment on your face, that I knew I made a mistake."

"Before anything could've been said, you just ran away. I am so sorry for intruding in your private moment and scaring you. I feel really awful about it, and I just wanted to come over here and let you know that." Completing her speech, Mrs. Hamilton rested her hands on her lap, and awaited the girl's response. Elizabeth hung on for dear life to every word that dropped from Samantha's lips. When she was finished, Elizabeth exhaled loudly, and looked down at her feet.

"Ummm…. Not too long after my mom and dad died, and I came here, I tried to make friends but it was hard for me and it didn't always work out. For years, people chose to adopt my friends and over and over again, I would be left feeling all alone. The other friends I made didn't really understand me, so I decided to stop with the friendships. After this decision, I would draw, paint, or write a poem to express myself, and it always worked to help me feel better."

"I can express myself in any way I want, without someone laughing at me, or mocking, criticizing or judging me. My pencils, paper, and paint will never abandon, hurt, or betray me like others have done." Elizabeth paused a little and then continued saying, "My art is all I have left in this world that makes me feel like I am a part of something. I have never let anyone see it because I don't want to be laughed at, or become the joke of the school."

"When you saw me yesterday, I felt so…exposed, and I was afraid that you would laugh at me and tell others, who would laugh at me too." Mrs. Hamilton noticed the sadness on the girl's face and the breaking of her voice, followed by a tear that Elizabeth quickly wiped away on the sleeve of her pajama shirt. She broke the weight of the moment by saying, "You know what? Go get dressed, and let's go for a walk to the new ice-cream shop a few blocks from here."

"Would that be okay?" Elizabeth smiled and nodded profusely, in agreement to the proposition. "Ice-cream makes everything better," she thought to herself, which was something that her mom used to say. Mrs. Hamilton rose from the chair to leave the room. When she was through the door, she turned around and said, "You have a rare gift and even though I wasn't supposed to see it, I am glad I did," she said, smiling a little.

"Meet me in the cafeteria when you are finished." With this, she turned around and made her way to the cafeteria. Elizabeth then closed the door, leaned against it, and tried to make sense of all that just happened. She then smiled to herself, satisfied with the fact that the misfortune of yesterday turned out well after all. The thought that Dean Hamilton was waiting for her in the cafeteria suddenly entered her mind and with this, she quickly ran to her bathroom to get ready for what that day was about to bring.

✻✻✻

Chapter Seven

Ice-Cream and Conversation

Elizabeth hurried down the stairs and headed to the cafeteria, to meet an eager but patient Mrs. Hamilton. "Are you ready?" Mrs. Hamilton asked gently as Elizabeth approached her. Elizabeth excitedly nodded in agreement. On their way to the ice-cream shop, Mrs. Hamilton asked a lot of questions including how her stay at the orphanage had been. Elizabeth explained that the experience at the orphanage had been good thus far, but she had no friends and no parents, and that made her feel all alone.

"There are so many children at the orphanage. You don't have any friends at all?" Mrs. Hamilton asked. Elizabeth suddenly remembered Stephan and said, "Stephan says he is my friend, best friend sometimes, but I don't know why he even says that. He is really good at everything and he has so much friends already, especially girls, but he hangs out with me for whatever reason. I think he feels sorry for me."

"I don't see the point in making any more friends or getting close to anyone else, because I lost everyone I was close to," Elizabeth explained. "I once had a daughter," Mrs. Hamilton began suddenly. "Eleven years ago, we were all in an accident that claimed the life of my beautiful little girl. She was eight years old at that time. Five years ago, my father died from a massive heart attack. He was my favorite person in this world, the best dad a child could ask for, and he was taken from me."

"The orphanage was his dream actually. You see, my dad didn't have a lot of money growing up but he was intelligent. His parents couldn't afford to send him to special schools to advance himself, so he went to regular schools where he excelled at everything. He was really good at cooking and baking, so he used this gift and sold baked goods. He used the money he made to buy supplies for school and books to teach himself everything he was able to learn."

"He worked hard and went on to college to study

business. He became a well-known businessman years later, opened bakeries, and invested in stocks. My mom said that he always told her that he didn't want his wife and children to struggle the way he and his parents did, so he worked hard to provide for my mom and I. He gave back a lot to communities, especially the ones similar to where he grew up. His dream was to work hard to give to those less fortunate than himself, especially children, and he made his dream a reality."

"He wanted children to have the opportunities he didn't have as a child, so he built a school for the gifted, where children who don't have enough money, can enroll and still get the best education in the arts, sports and many other areas. These children are tutored and well taken care of, and go to share their talent with the word. They put their heads together, and raise funds every year through different means such as concerts, for items for the school that they take care of together."

"He built and maintained parks in less fortunate areas so that children could still find joy in little ways, despite their family's unfortunate circumstances. The last idea my dad had was the orphanage. We worked on this together, just him and I mainly. He knew I loved children as much as he did, and we shared the same dream, so we worked together and built the orphanage into what it is today."

"My daughter was four at the time the orphanage opened, and enjoyed visiting and playing with the children here at the time. This was his last project before he died. This orphanage is fifteen years old, and every child in it is so dear to me, especially since I am unable to have any more." "Why can't you have any more children Dean Hamilton? Do you mind me asking?" Elizabeth asked, being careful not to upset her.

"No, I don't mind," Mrs. Hamilton replied. "After I had my daughter, I had to undergo emergency surgery. In the process, the doctors had no choice but to remove my ovaries, which has since prevented me from having children." Elizabeth, trying to make the conversation less uncomfortable said, "I see. It would seem like to you have a lot of money Dean Hamilton. Why are you working at the orphanage?"

"You can travel the world and vacation anywhere you like." Mrs. Hamilton smiled at the idea the child had. She then said, "You see, it has always been my passion to help children. I would rather stay here, work here, and be among you guys than anywhere else in the world, because this is my purpose. Besides, I have a very supportive husband who encourages my vision, and we both take the time to travel at least once a year, mainly to visit his parents in Australia."

"What's your husband's job? If you don't mind me asking," Elizabeth asked, hoping she wouldn't mind. "I don't mind at all. He is a Pediatric Surgeon. We met in high school where he was the classic captain of the football team, but he was also head of the science club. I loved science, so I joined the club and pretty soon, we became good friends. We later ended up in the same University where I majored in Child Psychology, and he was studying Medicine."

"We maintained our friendship and as time passed, we got really close and got married at twenty-five years old." Mrs. Hamilton smiled as she reminisced on these memories. At this point, they arrived at the ice-cream shop. They entered, had a seat, and gave their order to the waitress. "You are so lucky Dean Hamilton. You are a nice person, beautiful, rich and you have a good husband and mother. I wish I could be that lucky."

With this statement, Elizabeth looked uncomfortable. Mrs. Hamilton reached across the table and held the child's hands in hers. "You are staying in a great orphanage with people who truly care for you. You will get adopted by a very nice family, and you will go on to be one of the greatest persons I know, because your talent will make room for you and bring you before great men and women. I believe that."

"You are a beautiful girl as well, and one day you will meet a great guy who loves you unconditionally, and who shares and supports your dream. I know you will also have friends who will love and support you, but you have to let go of the fear of uncertainty. Instead, embrace what is happening in the present. Sad things happen every day. People's hearts get broken by family, friends, and loved ones but they learn and grow from it."

"Where would the world be if everyone was afraid to meet new people, and do things because of their fears? Learn from the past, bask in the present, and embrace the future, no matter what you are faced with," Mrs. Hamilton said. Tears started to well up in Elizabeth's eyes at these words. She was so inspired by the words spoken by such a powerful woman, who saw and understood her. They both smiled at each other, and Elizabeth thanked her for all that she said.

"No, thank you Elizabeth," Mrs. Hamilton replied. Elizabeth looked confused. "Why are you thanking me?" Elizabeth asked. "Because," Mrs. Hamilton began, "you reminded me of the reason behind why I started this journey in the beginning, and you made me recognize my true sense of purpose, even among the two people that I lost that were near and dear to me. So thank you." They both smiled, and were startled by the waitress putting their ice-cream before them.

They ate and spoke, and from that moment, because of that conversation, Elizabeth decided that she would think more about what her purpose on earth was. She also decided that she was going to try to make some friends by giving people a chance to get to know her and vice versa, instead of blocking them out entirely.

Chapter Eight

***

The Question

As they were on their way back to the orphanage, Elizabeth
tried to say something, but she kept stammering because she
didn't know how to start. Eventually, she managed to start
saying, "Dean Hamilton?" Mrs. Hamilton, alarmed by the way
in which the child stammered asked, "What's wrong?"
"Ummm," Elizabeth said as she looked uncomfortable. She
didn't know how Mrs. Hamilton would react to what she was
about to say.

She then closed her eyes, took a deep breath and asked,
"Can you be my mentor? I have never met anyone in real life
that is so awesome and inspiring. People look at movies once
and decide that an actor or actress will be their role model. The

reality is that these actors and actresses are out of our reach, but here you are. Just yesterday I was trying to avoid you, but so much has happened within the past few hours, that I don't want to waste time anymore."

"I now feel like I wasted time blocking people out, and never giving them a chance to teach me and learn from me to some extent. I have learnt so much from you today. So much so, that you inspired me to push myself and become more of who I am meant to be. I don't know my sole purpose yet, but I will figure it out, I know that. In a sense, you are better than a celebrity, and I want to continue to learn from you."

"You don't have to be my mom or guardian or anything like that, I cannot ask that of you. Conversations like the one we had today is all I ask for." Mrs. Hamilton, pleasantly surprised by the point made by the teenager before her, smiled, hugged the child, and said, "It would be an honor to be the role model for such a talented person." Elizabeth smiled and hugged Mrs. Hamilton back, feeling a sense of relief in knowing that a new chapter in her life had just begun.

Chapter Nine

✳ ✳ ✳

The Deal

"Adopt?!" David exclaimed, as he sprang from the living room sofa. "Isn't there some type of protocol against this since you are part of the orphanage?" Sam remained seated in her original position, which was next to him, and said, "It will not affect us. I own the orphanage." He then slowly walked toward Sam and stood in front of her before saying, "Look, I know it has been hard losing our little girl but another child will not replace-"

Before he could finish his sentence, Sam quickly stood up and said angrily, "You think I am making this decision because I want to replace Ana? No one will ever replace our daughter. She is the reason why we help so many children, teach them, mold them, protect them on a daily basis, so don't you dare think that I want to replace the memory of my daughter with another little girl! How dare you even think that David!"

Tears started to stream down Sam's face, upset by her husband's unfinished sentence. David, uncomfortable at the sight of his upset wife, hugged her as she sobbed with her face in his chest. "I'm sorry honey," he said gently. "I didn't mean to upset you. You love Anastasia, we both do. I know that you will never want to replace her. I am sorry for even thinking that you would want to do something like that."

Sam began to calm down but, with her face still buried in his chest, she apologized for shouting at him. He chuckled and said, "I deserved that so there is no need for an apology." After a few minutes of calming silence, David said, "Hey, can we make a deal?" Sam stopped hugging her husband and gazed intently at him, curious about what this deal would entail. "Let us wait a little while. I think maybe a year and a half at most."

"It will give us the time to be sure that we are not just going on emotions. We will get to know her more, and if we BOTH agree that this is what we really want to do, then we will start the process to legally adopt her." She stared at him, deep in thought, and eventually said, "Sounds fair enough. I think a new chapter in her life is just starting anyway and I really don't want to complicate it, especially if we are both not on the same page."

"Exactly. I would also like to meet this little girl who you are head over heels in love with," David said with a playful grin. Sam laughed and replied, "You will meet her whenever you're ready. She is such a sweetheart, with so much talent." "I bet she is but remember our deal, okay?" David said, trying to stare sternly at his wife without laughing. "One and a half years," she said, trying to look serious. David finally laughed because of the expression on Sam's face.

He then gave her a hug and kissed her forehead, as she hugged him back.

52

C h a p t e r   T e n

*** * ***

Elizabeth's Transformation

After her conversation with Mrs. Hamilton, Elizabeth became a little more social at first, and then felt comfortable enough to be a lot more social. She participated in a number of group projects with students of varying ages, throughout the orphanage. She opened up to a guidance counselor who helped her through her emotional struggles, and who also helped her along the path of loving herself. She made a lot of new friends of varying ages as well.

She became a better friend to Stephan by spending time with him and checking up on him, just like he would usually do for her on a daily basis. She even allowed him to watch her draw and write on early mornings and this seemed to be a delight to him. At times, she would catch glimpses of him staring at her instead of her art, and she would smile a little which would make him smile as well. She became more open with her art and poems by allowing people to view her pieces at various events, and by participating in Spoken Word competitions, where she became well known for her poems and her original point of view.

She continued to speak to Mrs. Hamilton, and they would have ice-cream and conversation every week. It became like a practice between them; their weekly ritual. One day, Elizabeth visited Mrs. Hamilton in her office. She knocked gently on the door and waited until she was given a verbal response to enter. Mrs. Hamilton was pleasantly surprised to see the child. She asked to what she owed the honor of her unforeseen visit, and Elizabeth said, "My birthday is this Sunday."

Mrs. Hamilton smiled and said, "I know." It is usually the custom for children who are celebrating a birthday at the orphanage, to suggest what they would like to do beforehand, and at the end of the activity, they would be treated to cake, ice-cream, and treat bags filled with goodies. Every child received this no matter their age, and they would all enjoy it every time. The kids were very adventurous with their ideas which ranged from costume parties, to water park fun.

Some would even suggest a charitable act. Because there were so many children and ideas, there were multiple parties per month which they thoroughly enjoyed. Over the years, Elizabeth had stopped making requests. She would just have the classic birthday party in the auditorium, but nothing exciting. Elizabeth's request this year, was to visit one of the parks built by Mrs. Hamilton's father. Mrs. Hamilton, a little taken aback by such a request, agreed.

She thought it would make her feel closer to her father, and grant her a slice of serenity just being wrapped up in another piece of his work. So that Sunday, Elizabeth and Mrs. Hamilton drove to the park, taking in every second of their journey. When they arrived, they slowly walked to and sat on the swings. Mrs. Hamilton closed her eyes, inhaled deeply, and smiled as she exhaled. It felt good being in the warm sun, feeling the gentle breeze brush against her face, almost caressing her face.

"I have to apply for college soon," Elizabeth blurted out, breaking Mrs. Hamilton's concentration. "I know," she responded with a smile, but Elizabeth looked anxious. "What's the matter Elizabeth?" At this point, Mrs. Hamilton gazed intently at the child as she felt alarmed by her expression. "I feel confused," she began. "After your talk with me a few months ago, I was led out of my comfort zone."

"I made friends, I entered competitions and won, I feel more positive and like a whole new person, but now I feel like everything is happening so fast. I have graduation coming up soon. I know it is a year from now but it still feels like soon to me, because it is my turn to leave along with the new friends I made in my year. I have part-time job offers to think about, I have colleges to research, and I really really like a boy who is getting adopted tomorrow."

"Why does this happen every time I get close to someone?" Mrs. Hamilton was nodding at each point until she heard about the boy Elizabeth liked. "Stephan?!" Mrs. Hamilton asked. She was aware of Stephan's adoption because she, along with a few members that make up her team, were in charge of all ongoing adoptions. Stephan turned sixteen years old as of recently, but even though he was older than Elizabeth, he was held back for some time due to anxiety he experienced at the end of his grade.

He received necessary counseling and his recovery took some time, but it went well. When he resumed classes, his new grade was with Elizabeth's class. However, he was graduating with Elizabeth the next year, and had already started planning for college. His dream is to become an engineer, and the couple adopting him were well accomplished but could never have a child, despite trying for years. Stephan was not exactly a child, but the couple preferred him since they were getting older and thought it would be nice to have someone older around, who could help them where necessary and vice versa.

Even though they were getting a child transitioning from high school to college, they were happy with their decision. Stephan's remarkable achievements caught their attention, and they seemed supportive of his career choice. Usually, all prospective adoptees would spend a day with their prospective parents, and Stephan seemed pleased with them after he spent time getting to know them better.

Because of his accomplishments, he would most likely receive a scholarship to pursue his course of study. There was no way Mrs. Hamilton knew that Elizabeth was interested in him, although she never really doubted that it was bound to happen. Elizabeth and Stephan competed in everything, most times against each other, but they always maintained their close friendship after all competitions came to an end.

"Elizabeth, look at me," Mrs. Hamilton said. "I know Stephan is your friend and you truly care about him, but this is not the end of anything. Children these days have different forms of communication, so nothing is going to stop you from communicating with him. Every child in this orphanage has a common goal and that is to get adopted. This is a new chapter in Stephan's life, and I think since you are his best friend, he needs your love and support the most."

"Everything will be alright dear," Mrs. Hamilton consoled. She took Elizabeth's hand in hers and smiled. Elizabeth in turn, gave a little smile, internalizing all that Mrs. Hamilton said. "Have you decided what you would like to study, and with what college? Let me guess? Is it Art?" Mrs. Hamilton asked, trying to change the subject. "Actually," Elizabeth began, "I would like to be an architect." This pleasantly surprised Mrs. Hamilton.

"This is great news! Have you had time to contemplate fully, to know that this is what you want?" Mrs. Hamilton asked. "Yes I know that this is what I want. I know that there is a lot more incorporated in the field of architecture, not just the beauty and uniqueness of each structure. In fact, architects are responsible for the strength of each structure and the lives of everyone that enters, which I think makes them very meticulous," Elizabeth said.

"Each building is a work of art, and an expression of the architect. I have been thinking this over and doing much research for a little while now, and I know that this is what I want." Mrs. Hamilton gave Elizabeth's hand a little squeeze, as she was filled with pride at the words of the person she came to love and see, as her own daughter. "I am so proud of you," Mrs. Hamilton said, as Elizabeth smiled at her.

59

Chapter   Eleven

❋❋❋

Surprise!

When they got back to the orphanage, Mrs. Hamilton took Elizabeth's hand, and they both headed toward her favorite place of serenity; overlooking the football field. "I want you to see how beautiful the sunset is from here," she said. As they approached the bench, the orange skies seemed to paint the entire area in its glow. It was breathtaking! Elizabeth closed her eyes and smiled, as she allowed the evening sunset to give her it's final warmth and goodbye until the next day.

Suddenly, her concentration was shattered by a loud, "SURPRISE!" She quickly opened her eyes, and saw all her friends and members of staff appear seemingly out of nowhere, with birthday hats, cake, and confetti! It was a beautiful sight!

Her friends hugged her one at a time, and then in groups. Mrs. Hamilton looked on smiling, as she was touched by the amount of love this once friendless child had gained in the matter of months.

"You did well with her," a voice said from behind. She spun around to see David walking toward her with a big grin on his face. "What a pleasant surprise. I wonder who invited my husband to this event?" she asked jokingly, while looking at her assistant Melissa. "I will be right back," Melissa said, and she quickly walked away. "I had to come see the child that has influenced my wife and vice versa, from what I've heard", David said.

"Oh?" began Mrs. Hamilton, "and what have you heard?" He smiled and answered, "I heard stories of a fourteen-year-old little girl who was very shy, awkward, and isolated but in the matter of a few months, became confident, happy, and more involved in social activities, after spending time with my wife. It is kind of like a movie actually." Samantha laughed. "I see," she said, "would you like to meet her?"

Before David could answer, she took his hand in hers, and led the way to introduce him to Elizabeth. As David was being introduced to the child, he was astonished to think that she was the same child everyone was talking about. She was not shy at all and was very polite. "Happy birthday Elizabeth. It is nice to finally meet you. Would you like to walk with me? I want to get to know the child my wife has become so fond of."

With this, the child smiled. Jokingly gesturing for David to lead the way, she said, "Shall we?" "We shall," David replied, chuckling as he played along. With this, they went off talking. Samantha watched them as they seemed to talk about so many things. She was curious to know exactly what was being said. There were moments where they looked solemn, and moments where you could see the expression of excitement emanating from the child.

Samantha was pleasantly surprised with what she was witnessing before her. Finally, David and Elizabeth rejoined her at the same spot where they were introduced. "It was a pleasure Elizabeth. You and my wife need to invite me to one of your get-togethers. It sounds like you both have a lot of fun," David said smiling at the child. "You will have to ask Dean Hamilton, but I don't think she'll mind," Elizabeth replied, grinning at Mrs. Hamilton.

Elizabeth then left the two alone, as she caught a glimpse of Stephan in a corner by himself. "I now see why you are fond of her. She is quite an awesome child. She has had a difficult past but she is so full of life and excitement," David said, smiling to himself. "Mr. Hamilton, we have not reached our full year- and- a- half agreement yet, and you seem to want to adopt the child on the spot," Samantha said, as she smirked at David.

"She is a really nice girl, and I am even more in awe that you helped her so much. I am so proud of you. I can now truly say that I am on board with her adoption, but I really do want to spend time with you guys on your little ice-cream dates." Samantha laughed and hugged her husband, quite pleased that he finally met the child that changed her life.

Chapter Twelve

✳ ✳ ✳

Stephan's Confession

"Hi Stephan, what's up?" Elizabeth asked, smiling as she approached a very nervous looking Stephan. This was unlike him. "As you know, I am getting adopted tomorrow," Stephan started. Elizabeth's smile faded, as she told him that she knew. "What I am about to tell you, I don't think you know already though. I am excited that I am going to a real home with real parents and a family, but the one thing I will miss every day is spending time with you."

Elizabeth's eyes widened with surprise at his confession. "I sometimes catch myself staring and smiling whenever you talk to me. I internalize every word you say, how you say it, and the very sound of your voice cheers me up in an instant. I have liked you since we met, and I dare say in this moment that I think I am in love with you. I know we're young and don't know a thing about love but I know how I feel about you and that is why I choose to use the word 'love'."

"I hope I am not making a fool of myself because I don't know if you feel the same way, but I had to tell you before I leave. I will still attend school here because my new parents don't think it would do any good to transfer me to another school now, since I have one more year left here. So we will still see each other at school. Please don't hesitate to call or text me for anything at all okay?" Elizabeth's face turned a bright red.

She couldn't find any words, and she knew she was about to cry. She nodded in agreement at his request. Stephan gently took both her hands in his and said, "You make me better. You are my friend, my best friend right now, but one day I hope that we can be more than that, but only when you are ready. I really do hope you feel the same way. If not, I just made myself look like an idiot." Elizabeth's words still failed her.

She threw her arms around his neck, and cried softly as he hugged her back. "You are not an idiot because I feel the same way about you," she said softly in his ear as she continued hugging him. He smiled to himself as he hugged her tightly. He found comfort in knowing that she liked him as well, and he did not just look like an idiot in front of the girl he loved.

Chapter Thirteen

***

Elizabeth's Progression

Time seemingly flew past. The semesters came and went, and with it, Elizabeth continued to grow and learn so much from those around her. Mrs. Hamilton would feel proud when witnessing her in competitions, and hearing her speak so eloquently. This was a vast improvement from the girl she first met. Elizabeth was almost sixteen now and even more beautiful. She was slender, with her hair even longer than before but now, it was not hidden in a bun under a hoodie.

She would sometimes leave it loose with only a headband, or she would put it up in a ponytail, allowing her curls falling past her shoulders and down her back. Her style of dressing also changed from jeans and tees only, to adding sneaker dresses, blouses, skirts, and shorts on occasion, to her wardrobe. Her love for the arts and reading never dwindled, no matter how much time passed. She gained a love for fashion, shoes, and design, especially that of buildings.

Mrs. Hamilton sat and admired how the child had grown. "Are you having the same flavor or are you trying something new today?" Her chain of thought was suddenly broken by Elizabeth's question. They were in their usual ice-cream shop, having an early celebration of Elizabeth's graduation. "I'll have chocolate mint dear," Mrs. Hamilton said, smiling at her. Elizabeth asked Mrs. Hamilton if she was okay because she seemed spaced out.

She took Elizabeth's hands in hers and said, "I am just so proud of the person you have become. Look at you! You have grown up and become even more beautiful and graceful than when I first met you. It has been a little over a year since our encounter at the football field. I can never forget the first time I saw you; the awkward fourteen-year-old girl, perched on the bench, caught up in her own world. I never thought that I would be looking at you right now, so grown up."

Elizabeth gently squeezed Mrs. Hamilton's hands. "I have you to thank. You say that I am as beautiful as I am graceful, but how I really feel is grateful. Grateful that you took the time to teach me and groom me into who I am today. I would've never discovered my true potential if it wasn't for you. I would've never discovered who I wanted to become if it wasn't for your patience, care, and love. Today, my art is known, and my voice has been heard through my poems because of you."

"I thank God everyday for you and Mr. Hamilton. I always pray that you both are blessed with your heart's desires because of what you both have done for me. I will never forget, and I want you to believe that." Mrs. Hamilton smiled at the child and bit her lip to stop herself from releasing the tears that were to come. Having composed herself, she managed to thank Elizabeth and said, "Let's finish this ice-cream and head back early."

"You need an early night for tomorrow."

72

Chapter Fourteen

***

Unexpected Information

"Today is the day you have been waiting for! Are you ready?" Mrs. Hamilton asked as she poked her head through Elizabeth's bedroom door. Elizabeth was nervously trying to fix her hair when Mrs. Hamilton greeted her with the question. "If my hands can stop shaking enough to fix this bun," Elizabeth retorted as she struggled in front of the mirror to get her hair the way she wanted. Mrs. Hamilton quickly entered the room to help Elizabeth, who seemed relieved by her gesture.

"Were you this nervous for your graduation?" Elizabeth asked. Mrs. Hamilton seemingly reminisced to her graduation day, smiled, and said, "Yes, actually. It is a big step in a person's life. It represents their years of hard work that has finally paid off, and it also represents transitioning from one level to another." "I am scared of the transition. I don't know exactly what the next level holds, so it is nerve-wracking," Elizabeth admitted, obviously nervous.

Mrs. Hamilton, not wanting the child to panic said, "Your emotions are understood, but I need you to breathe and let's take this one step at a time." "We will get over this part first, then move on to the next step after this day is completed, agreed?" "Agreed," said Elizabeth, who inhaled slowly and deeply, and exhaled in order to calm her nerves. The two ladies were startled by a knock on the door. To their surprise, Mr. Hamilton opened the door a little, and peeked nervously through.

"Honey, what are you doing here?!" Mrs. Hamilton asked, obviously surprised. "I have something to share with the both of you," he said in a solemn tone. He slowly walked over to his wife, kissed her and then stooped in front of Elizabeth. He took the girl's hand and said, "My wife has never stopped talking about you since the day she met you with your art. You have made her life and mine so much better just by being present and by being yourself."

"We lost our daughter a long time ago as you may know by now, and we have never forgotten her to this day. After you told me your story on your birthday, I did some digging and I found out that both your family and mine were involved in the same accident. That same accident that claimed the lives of your parents and our daughter. The truth is that the rain was pouring heavily that day. I remember that part vividly because Ana was singing, 'rain rain go away'."

The brakes in your parents' car malfunctioned, so they switched on their caution lights and police believed that your parents tried to pull aside and either have the car slow down on its' own, or use the hand brakes to stop it completely. Unfortunately, a truck sped up in order to not get the red light, and in that process, it hit your parents' car, which was pulling into that lane in order to get aside safely. Their car skidded, hit a pole, and was thrown into our lane, crashing into our vehicle."

"You escaped with minor bruising and scratches, which was a miracle because of the extent of the damage to your parents' vehicle, but your parents were not that fortunate. My wife didn't know about your situation because she was not present here for months after the accident. When you came to this orphanage, I am not sure if anyone really knew that you were the child involved in the same accident as us. I never looked into the full story because I had so much on my plate, and as time passed, I never thought it made sense to look into it because the loss of our daughter was too much."

"I'm so sorry that I had to tell you this today but I didn't think it was right to withhold it from you for another minute." Mrs. Hamilton placed her hands over her mouth and quietly sobbed at this revelation. "My wife has never been herself since that day, but when you came into her life, there was joy in her heart for the first time in a very long time. She laughed more, she joked more, she was more like herself before we lost our daughter."

"Our daughter had so much love in her heart for everyone, and I think if she was alive today and met you, she would've loved you the way we do. So today, I am asking on behalf of my wife and myself, if you would like to be a part of our family." Tears streamed down Elizabeth's face as she tried to make sense of everything she had just heard. It was too much to interpret and yet, she felt like she got the closure she was seeking concerning what happened that day.

The smell of the rain, the ambulance, the screams, it all made sense now. Her parents died in the same crash that claimed the daughter of the person she admired?! This was all so strange, and with all of what was just said, they still wanted to adopt her? This was insane! She couldn't find her words, so she lunged forward and hugged Mr. Hamilton, crying on his shoulder. He then reached out one hand to his wife, and gently pulled her into their group hug, as she couldn't seem to stop crying.

C h a p t e r F i f t e e n

✳ ✳ ✳

Graduation!

"Elizabeth Adams," retorted the speaker. Cheers went up and continued until she was on the stage. "Continue to do great things and make us all proud," her principal whispered to her as she collected her diploma and shook her hand. "Thank you," she replied as she smiled back at her. She turned to the crowd, and lifted her diploma into the air with a big grin on her face. Everyone cheered even louder, especially Mr. and Mrs. Hamilton, who gave her two thumbs up in the crowd.

It all felt like a dream. Everything seemed to move in slow motion from the moment she began to walk off the stage. After the ceremony, Elizabeth and her friends were signing each other's yearbooks. There was much hugging, tears of joy, and words of encouragement, as the teenagers cherished their last moments together. "You look beautiful," a voice said from behind Elizabeth, as she was having a conversation with some girls from the Drama Club.

She spun around and saw Stephan! She wrapped her arms around his neck, as he lifted her into the air and spun her. "I am so happy to see you! You missed the ceremony Stephan Kai," she told him as she playfully hit his arm. "I know I am late, but of course I will not miss the opportunity to see my beautiful girlfriend close this chapter of her life," Stephan replied. With this, Elizabeth blushed. "Thank you, now go collect your diploma," Elizabeth said laughing, as she gently pushed Stephan away.

"Why didn't you tell me anything?" Mrs. Hamilton asked her husband as they sat down at a table in the hall. "I didn't know anything at all about the accident, and I also had no idea that we had reached an agreement concerning Elizabeth's adoption. You gave me one and a half years David! We still have a few months left." David, feeling somewhat guilty about the whole ordeal said, "I know honey but when Elizabeth told me her story, it haunted me so much, that I felt like I needed to learn more."

"So I got Keith to investigate further, and he only gave me

the full file this morning. After I read everything in it, I decided to come down here and explain everything to you and Elizabeth. Everything was in it; from the cause of the accident, to the victims. In almost the year that I have known Elizabeth, I have grown to love her as if she was our own child. I finally understood why you wanted to adopt her so badly."

"We have learnt so much from each other, and even though you and your dad have made this orphanage like a home for these children, nothing can beat the reality of having a family who loves and cares for them. I needed an unbiased view on the entire situation, so I spoke to your mom and both my parents at length. When we were finished, my final take on it was that we should legally adopt her. I wanted it all to be a surprise for you."

"I knew you were already on board, so I handled all the paperwork. All that's left now is an interview." "Oh honey, you did all of those things already?" Sam asked, a little disappointed that she wasn't part of the process. "Yeah, you're not having second thoughts are you?" David asked. "Of course not. I am so overwhelmed right now. I hardly know how to feel or what to think. Today is truly a great day," she replied, comforted by the fact that things had worked out so well.

"I just have to wait on Joyce to speak to the social worker

concerning if she can stay with us prior to the interview. I have not received a date yet for it," David added. "Honey, I am the owner of the orphanage, how is it that I knew nothing?" Sam asked, completely puzzled by the undermining by her staff. "Because honey, you are not the one in charge of THIS adoption," David laughed. "You had this all worked out, and you even got Joyce to tell me nothing about it?"

Sam asked as she started putting together the entire scenario in her head. David replied, "I asked her to keep it that way unless there was anything that required your input, like legal matters. Only then, I would've told you sooner. I have Nathan on top of that too." "You brought in our lawyer? This is an entire team David!" Sam exclaimed shocked. Her husband patiently replied, "I want to be sure that we have everything in order so that we have no hiccups."

"Once Elizabeth comes home with us, she is our child, and I don't want anything to go wrong." Sam, touched by the thought put into the entire process by David replied, "Honey, I don't even know what to say except thank you." "You don't need to thank me because this is our journey," he replied as he smiled at her. At this moment, David's phone rang. "It's Joyce," he whispered as he stepped away from the table to take the phone call.

"Hi Joyce," he greeted her. "Good evening Dr. Hamilton. I am sorry to disturb you as I am aware that you are most likely at the Graduation Dinner," Joyce started. "It's no problem at all. It is important because it concerns Elizabeth. How is everything?" David asked. "Well sir," she continued, "I am pleased to report that the paperwork process for Elizabeth's adoption is almost completed. All that I would need on one final document is your signature, and that of Mrs. Hamilton."

"Your interview has been scheduled for this Monday, but I managed to have the option open for if you both would like to conduct it this evening. I understand that the process has been a long and tedious one…," "Of course. We can do the interview today since we are already on the compound," David interrupted, too excited to make sense of what he was saying. "Good," Joyce said pleased. "I will call you back after I have gathered everyone and everything needed for the interview."

"A common question asked is if the child can stay with the prospective parents prior to the final interview being conducted, and yes that can happen, once the parents and environment has been cleared by one of our social workers. Once the interview goes well, she can go home with you both immediately if that is your wish." "I don't think it would be wise to take her tonight if everything goes well, because it would already be too late at night to ask her to organize everything."

"We will see how the interview goes, and then we will be able to update her from there. If all goes well, we will pick her up here tomorrow and give you the final signed document," David replied. "No problem at all Dr. Hamilton. I will contact you when we are ready," Joyce replied. "Thank you Joyce. I will give Mrs. Hamilton the good news, and we will see you in a little while." David then hung up the phone and walked back to the table, where a very excited Mrs. Hamilton asked, "What did she say?"

"She said that she has managed to get our interview for this evening. If the interview is successful, we will be able to take Elizabeth home as soon as we sign the final paperwork. We will need to update Elizabeth and let her know that she can be home with us as soon as tomorrow. We will also have to sign and give the final document to Joyce once we pick her up."

"I pray to God that everything works out in our favor," David said, grabbing and gently squeezing Sam's hand. "Oh my gosh, I don't know if my heart can take any more of this. I feel like this is all a dream coming true," Samantha said. "As I said, this is a new journey for us all. We don't know what lies ahead, but I know that it is going to be beautiful," David said as Sam looked at him nervously. Suddenly, David's phone rang.

It was Joyce. "Hi Dr. Hamilton, we are ready." "Thank you Joyce, we will be right there," he said and hung up the phone. He stood up, took the hand of a very nervous Samantha Hamilton, and together they went to their interview.

✳✳✳

Adoption!

"I have news for you, Stephan!" Elizabeth exclaimed, failing to hide her excitement. The two were now seated and having dinner in the hall, when Elizabeth brought up her exciting news. "Oh yeah? What is it?" Stephan asked, curious to know the source of her excitement. "I am going to be adopted by Mr. and Mrs. Hamilton!" she exclaimed, grinning from ear to ear. Stephan's jaw dropped open, almost spilling the food that just went into his mouth.

"Stephan, are you okay?" Elizabeth asked, startled by Stephan's reaction. Stephan shook his head to snap out of the trance he seemed to be in, got up quickly, and pulled Elizabeth into a hug. "You seem more excited than me Stephan," Elizabeth said giggling. "I prayed hard for this," he started. "I have experienced love from both my parents so far, and I hoped that you would experience that same love for yourself, and it has happened!"

"I am pleasantly surprised and majorly happy for you." "Thank you Stephan," Elizabeth said as she hugged him back. "Oh look, my parents are here. Let me introduce you," Stephan said as he glimpsed his parents over Elizabeth's shoulder. He put out his hand for Elizabeth's, who smiled and gladly put her hand in his. As they both stood together, he kissed her on the cheek, and they made their way across to where his parents were seated.

"Hi Stephan, sorry we're late," said Mr. Harris as he started eating. "Oh Derek, mind your manners. Stephan has brought someone. Never mind your father dear. Who is this beautiful young lady?" A very curious Glenda Harris asked. Glenda was tall and slender, with short, black, straight hair. She was of Spanish descent which was obvious by the accent she possessed. Her husband Derek was slightly shorter and thicker, with very short brown hair, and a cheerful disposition.

He seemed to light up the room with his cheerfulness. "Mom, dad, this is Elizabeth, my girlfriend. Remember I mentioned her to you? We have grown together in this orphanage, and she was my only friend when I didn't have one. She remained my friend even when I had many. The day before I left the orphanage, I told her how I felt and we have been together ever since," Stephan explained, smiling at the last part.

Mr. And Mrs. Harris stood up to greet Elizabeth. Mr. Harris shook her hand saying, "Nice to finally meet you Elizabeth. Steph really did tell us so much about you already. I can finally put a face to your name. It is great to know that our son has such a beautiful young lady like you as his girlfriend." Mrs. Harris, quite emotional after such an introduction, hugged Elizabeth and said, "It's so nice to finally meet you." Elizabeth smiled and hugged her back.

"Elizabeth found out today that she is going to be adopted......by the owner of the orphanage!" Stephan said excitedly. "That's wonderful news Elizabeth! Mrs. Hamilton has done so much to help us during the adoption process. Is she here?" Mrs. Harris asked, looking around the room for her. "Yes, she is here actually. If you want, I can take you to her." David and Samantha had recently returned from a very successful adoption interview, and were seated at their table for dinner.

Elizabeth, together with Stephan and his parents, all

walked across to Mr. and Mrs. Hamilton's table. "Is everything alright dear?" Mrs. Hamilton asked Elizabeth as she approached. "Derek, Glenda, Stephan, nice to see you all again. This is my husband, Dr. Hamilton. Honey, this is the lovely couple that adopted Stephan," Sam mentioned to David. "Oh I see, congratulations!" David said, standing and shaking their hands.

"Thank you sir, but I think congratulations are in order for you both, concerning the decision to adopt such a beautiful young lady," Mr. Harris returned. "Thank you," Mr. and Mrs. Hamilton replied simultaneously, then smiled at each other. "I have something to tell you both," Elizabeth started, "I was going to wait until a better time to tell you guys but I guess now is fine. Stephan is my boyfriend. He has been for a while now," she said.

Mr. Hamilton's eyes widened as he looked at a grinning Mrs. Hamilton who said, "Today is a day to celebrate indeed! Congratulations honey." She then stood up and hugged both Elizabeth and Stephan. "Congratulations," Mr. Hamilton said drily, as he shook Stephan's hand. "We're just going to finish up dinner and I think I will turn in for the night, but I will tell you both before I leave okay?" Elizabeth said.

"Sure honey," replied Mrs. Hamilton. "It was a pleasure to meet you all again," Samantha told Mr. and Mrs. Harris. "The pleasure was ours. Have a great evening," Glenda said smiling, as she and her husband shook the hands of the Hamiltons once more, and returned to their table. "Boyfriend?!" David whispered loudly after the kids and Stephan's parents left them. "Oh relax honey. They have known each other for years."

"Stephan is a really nice boy. I know because I have supervised them both and taught them over the years, so I can assure you that he is a nice boy," Sam calmly said to her husband. David seemed less tense after her reassurance. He said, "I trust you, but I will see for myself how nice he is." He then let out a sigh as he thought about Elizabeth's boyfriend confession, and said, "I hope he doesn't hurt her."

"She has been through enough already." "I hope not too honey," Sam replied, "but we cannot be controlling over her decisions." "We can't?" David asked jokingly. Sam stared at him with a stern look on her face. "Oh alright," he said, rolling his eyes as Samantha smiled at him. "Now that we are finished with high school, what are your plans? Have you applied for any colleges yet?" Elizabeth asked Stephan. "I applied to a few."

"I want to be an engineer so bad, so I am keeping my fingers crossed, hoping that I get accepted to at least one of the colleges I applied to," he replied. "I know you would," Elizabeth said reassuringly. "Thank you," Stephan said smiling as he held Elizabeth's hand on the table. "The last time we spoke about studies, you hadn't made your mind up about what you wanted to study. Have you figured it out?"

"Have you applied to any colleges?" Stephan asked. "I actually did both," Elizabeth answered. "I want to study architecture. I have applied to colleges that offer it, which isn't a whole lot, but I still have options. I am keeping my fingers crossed for MIT though." "Really?! That is one of my options as well!" exclaimed Stephan excitedly. "Wouldn't it be crazy cool if we both got in? We could make new friends, help each other out, and I promise you that I wouldn't be a clingy boyfriend."

Elizabeth laughed as Stephan said this. "I think it would be pretty cool too. I don't want to get my hopes too high though, so I am saving my excitement for when I hear back from them," Elizabeth said. "That is understandable, but you are one of the smartest persons I know, and you're equally talented, so I have no doubt that you would get in." Elizabeth blushed at Stephan's praise. "I am so tired. Can you walk me back to my room?" Elizabeth asked.

"Of course," Stephan said as he got up from his seat. "Let

me just tell Mr. and Mrs. Hamilton that I am going to turn in for the night," Elizabeth said. "Sure," Stephan replied, and they walked to where Mr. and Mrs. Hamilton were continuing their dinner. "Mr. and Mrs. Hamilton, I am heading up to my room now. Stephan is going to walk me there," Elizabeth said, exhaustion clearly evident in her voice as well as on her face.

Mr. Hamilton began to cough almost instantly. Mrs. Hamilton looked nervous as she listened to these words. Elizabeth hugged her and whispered, "Don't worry, I promise you that we are not going to do anything inappropriate." Mrs. Hamilton hugged her tighter and said, "Thank you." "Stephan, can you give me a second?" Elizabeth asked. "Of course," he replied. "I will go tell my folks that I will be right back."

With this, Stephan walked off to speak to his parents. "I just want to say something," Elizabeth started as Mr. and Mrs. Hamilton stared intently and curiously. "I grew up in this orphanage, barely remembering my parents, but graphically remembering what happened to them. Dean Hamilton, since you started mentoring me, you have been nothing but a blessing to me in so many ways. The both of you have given me hope for a better and brighter future, as well as so much love."

"I can never repay any of you for your kindness, but I hope

that my words of gratitude, and the love I have for you both will show that I am truly grateful for all that you have done for me so far. I have to keep trying to come back to reality because it seems like I am having a dream. Then I realize that my dream is being lived in real life, and tears come to my eyes because I never once thought that I would be living this life."

"I hope I do not disappoint you, as I aim to be the best that I can be. I am not here to replace your daughter. That is a void that can never be filled. I am just glad that you took the second shot at being parents, and you chose me to be a part of this awesome journey. So thank you." Mrs. Hamilton couldn't stop the tears at the girl's beautiful words. They both stood and hugged the child, who closed her eyes and hugged them back, as her heart filled with nothing but love for the both of them.

"We have something to tell you as well," Mr. Hamilton said. He then looked at his wife, hinting at her to deliver the good news. "Your adoption has been finalized so you can come home with us tomorrow," Mrs. Hamilton said smiling. Elizabeth could not hold back her joy. She burst into tears and Mr. and Mrs. Hamilton hugged her. After a while, they all let go of each other, and watched as Stephan came up to them smiling, took their daughter by the hand, and led her away as she told him the good news.

"Are you sure they aren't going to do anything? I have a teenage daughter now, so I am very nervous," David asked Sam. "She is going to be fine. I know them, and trust them," Sam replied. "Let's finish up dinner and head home. We have an exciting day tomorrow, and we would both need our energy." They both smiled at the thought that Elizabeth would be home with them tomorrow. They then sat down, and continued their dinner.

Chapter Seventeen

***

Final Night

"Are you asleep?" Stephan whispered to Elizabeth as they lay in her bed. Stephan lay on his side behind her, as she lay on her side wrapped in his arms. "How can I sleep if you keep asking me if I am asleep?" responded Elizabeth sleepily. "I'm sorry," chuckled Stephan. "It is just so unbelievable how everything is falling into place. I have been bracing myself for something bad to happen, but then my dad said if I keep living like that, I wouldn't be able to enjoy what is happening now, so I decided to live in the moment instead of worrying about what may or may not happen."

"Problems will arise, but we never need to live looking

forward to something bad happening. I am enjoying the now. I am here with the girl that I love, cuddled in her bed until she falls asleep. We both graduated today and we will both be heading to college soon, hopefully the same one. I thank God for raining his favor on me." At this, Stephan hugged Elizabeth tighter and whispered, "Are you asleep?"

No response. He smiled to himself, and slowly climbed out of the bed. He then draped a blanket over her, kissed her on the cheek, and left the room, staring at her one last time before he left. On his way back to the hall, he met Mr. and Mrs. Hamilton heading to the parking lot. "Mr. and Mrs. Hamilton!" he shouted, causing them both to spin around. He approached them and said, "Elizabeth is asleep. I want to assure you that nothing happened between us apart from talking."

"That's relieving Stephan, thank you for letting us know," Mrs. Hamilton responded, smiling at him. "Also," he continued, "I just want to let you know that I love your daughter. She means a lot to me, and I will not disrespect her or any of you in any way at all. What you both have done today has made her very happy, and I wish that she can remain that way forever. I just wanted to let you know that. Thank you both for a wonderful evening."

"I am going to find my parents and head home." Mrs.

Hamilton stepped forward and hugged Stephan. Mr. Hamilton patted him on his shoulder and congratulated him on graduation. He smiled at them both, and walked off to find his parents. Mrs. Hamilton stared at Mr. Hamilton with a pleased smirk on her face. "Ok," Mr. Hamilton said as he rolled his eyes, "he seems to be a nice boy like you said. That's our daughter now, a father worries."

"I know," said Mrs. Hamilton as she laughed and hugged her husband. "Let's go home." With this said, they both got into their car, and headed home.

***

Chapter Eighteen

Home At Last

"Are you excited?" Mrs. Hamilton asked Elizabeth nervously, while catching glimpses of her in the front passenger seat. "I am very excited. I just want to take in everything because I think apart from when I'm doing my art, this is the happiest I have ever been." Mrs. Hamilton smiled at the excited girl's remarks. Mrs. Hamilton pulled into a neighborhood that looked quite like the ones seen on TV; there were kids playing in the street as the warmth of the sun shone through trees and onto them.

There were orange leaves that decorated the front lawns of the houses, giving one the impression of an orange blanket draped on the lawn itself. Some children were seen playing in the orange leaves, enjoying it every way imaginable. The houses were even more beautiful. They were not exactly huge like mansions, but they were not small like cottages either. They were big and looked warm and cozy, just like home.

"Wow," the girl whispered to herself as they passed a row of big beautiful houses of varying colors. Mrs. Hamilton smiled and pulled into the driveway of a burgundy and white house. It was big and beautiful, with a huge front porch that had a swinging bench. The porch overlooked a green lawn to the left and right, separated by a burgundy and white brick pathway down the middle, that led to a white pedestrian gate.

On the right lawn stood a white three-tiered water fountain. There was a white cherubim inside the first tier which was on top. Engraved in this tier, were vines running around the circumference of it with leaves and flowers. The cherubim inside seemed to be pouring from a big vase. Out of this vase came the water for the fountain, which trickled down to the second tier that was in the shape of a lotus. Seated on the petals of the lotus, were little-sculpted fairies, that seemed to be playing in the falling water!

The third and final tier was big and round, with engravings of fairies playing with birds, and flowers surrounding them. It was beautiful! On the left lawn stood a bird bath. The bath was big and round. It was well supported by a white pillar-like structure, with markings all around it. It seemed to resemble a tree! Protruding from one side was a long branch that held a little bowl, and on the opposite side there was another branch that held another bowl.

Both bowls were slightly higher than the bath. Upon closer observation, one could see that one bowl held birdseed while the other bowl held drinking water. Some little birds were already playing happily in the bath! Mrs. Hamilton said, "We're home," unable to stop her voice from breaking. She was so overcome with joy, that she felt like crying but she fought back the tears. As they both stepped out of the car, Mr. Hamilton appeared from the garage that was situated up ahead in the driveway, at one end of the front of the house.

He wore a big smile on his face, and walked straight toward Elizabeth. "Welcome home," he said as he hugged her. He then went into the trunk to get Elizabeth's bag. She came with just a few items; a lot of books, sketch pads, and a few pieces of clothing, all packed into a small suitcase. As Elizabeth slowly walked toward the porch, the front door swung open and an aged woman stepped out wearing one of the biggest smiles Elizabeth had ever seen.

She looked just like Mrs. Hamilton but older! She was tall and slim with shoulder length, straight, grey hair. She was wearing white loafers, light blue tapered ankle pants with a white shirt tucked in, and a light blue cardigan draped over her shoulders, with the arms tied loosely and hanging at her chest. Elizabeth smiled nervously at the woman. "She is so beautiful!" the woman exclaimed. Mrs. Hamilton walked up behind Elizabeth and said, "Elizabeth, this is my mom, your new grandmother."

Elizabeth put her hand out to shake her new grandmother's hand, but she grabbed her and pulled her into a tight hug. "I am so happy you're here finally," she told Elizabeth. "I'm happy to be here," Elizabeth replied as she hugged her back. "Come honey, I'll show you to your room. Mom are you staying for dinner?" Samantha asked as they all entered the house. "No dear, I have to head home and pack for my trip to Rome," her mom replied.

Samantha's mom Nadine, was part of a club that traveled with people her age twice a year. This year, they were going to Rome for one week. "When I get back, I would like to spend some time with my granddaughter," Nadine said. Mrs. Hamilton laughed and replied, "Sure mom." At this time, Nadine's caregiver pulled into the driveway to take her back home.

"That's Sadie. I better get going," she said as she looked out the window.

She quickly hugged everyone, kissed Elizabeth on the forehead and said, "Welcome home dear. I will see you in one week." "Thank you. It was nice meeting you. Have a safe trip," Elizabeth replied smiling. She watched as her grandma walked out the front door, got into the car, and left with Sadie. The inside of the house was even more beautiful than the outside! Upon entering the house through the front door, you immediately stepped into an open area with a white staircase to the right.

On it lay a long burgundy carpet, leading all the way up the stairs. Beyond the staircase, was a wide oval doorway that led to the family room. The family room was huge! Navy blue carpet covered the entire area and on it was a long grey sofa in the shape of an 'L'. Each wall in this room was decorated with photographs and paintings as well as cascading shelves that held trophies and awards. To add to the excitement of the living room, all the seats of the sofa reclined with an armrest option between each seat.

Hanging on the wall in front of the sofa, was a huge curved television with an entertainment stand encasing it. The stand was equipped with different electronics including a surround sound system, gaming consoles and countless accompanying game disks. Along the wall of the entertainment stand, stood a door that led out of that room into another carpeted room. The carpet in this room was grey but the room itself had white walls decorated with framed paintings.

There was also a huge fireplace against one of the walls. It was painted in grey as well, but accented in white. On the mantle stood a few family photographs. There were baby blue and silver single chairs with little accent tables next to them, surrounding the fireplace. These tables and chairs were spaced out enough to form an open circle. There was a white bookshelf against one of the walls, that had seemingly countless books of varying topics and sizes.

Everything in the room was a beautiful baby blue, silver, grey, and white. This room seemed to be a little more formal. It looked like it was used for special guests or occasions. When you exited this room and re-entered the living room, you could see the kitchen and dining area situated directly behind it. The kitchen and dining area were a little more elevated. Three long vertical steps separated the elevated area from the living room area.

The kitchen was a beautiful red and white, with silver

cookware and utensils neatly put away. All the electronics were a beautiful balance of red, white, and silver as well. Running against the entire length of one of the kitchen walls were marble countertops, with a beautiful silver flat top stove and oven in the middle, evenly separating one set of countertops from another. Appliances were neatly placed on the countertops; a beautiful array if red and silver.

The refrigerator as well was red and silver, and stood after the final counter, seemingly bringing an end to the row of counters. An island ran parallel to the counters and had the same marble design. On one side of the island, overlooking the kitchen, were four red and silver bar stools. On the opposite end of the kitchen was a beautiful dining area, with an elegant black and gold rectangular table, surrounded by eight accompanying chairs.

The seats and backrests bore an almost Victorian style pattern. A chandelier with hanging crystals was perfectly placed in the middle of the ceiling, and hung directly over the table. The dining room setting gave one the feeling like that of a family dinner environment. There were glass sliding doors that led out of the kitchen and dining area onto an open porch. From the porch, you got a beautiful view of the backyard where the sun glistened off the water in a long, wide pool, which was surrounded by yellow and white striped lounge chairs.

The yard was decorated with a cabana, private bathrooms, showers, a bar, and a grilling station. The entire house was so beautiful, and every room was a masterpiece. Elizabeth was standing at the bottom of the staircase that led upward to a place unexplored. "Are you ready to see your room?" This question broke Elizabeth's concentration. She spun around to see Mr. and Mrs. Hamilton smiling at her.

She shook her head slowly, indicating yes. Mrs. Hamilton took her hand as Mr. Hamilton led the way up the staircase. Elizabeth felt like she was in a dream where everything moved in slow motion. They met a wide hallway at the top of the stairs, filled with photos and paintings on the white walls. There were a few doors on either side of the hallway, each leading to a new room. Mr. Hamilton stopped at a door on the right, turned around, and smiled at the two ladies.

He then opened the door gently. Still holding Elizabeth's hand, Mrs. Hamilton led Elizabeth into the room. Elizabeth's jaw dropped as she stepped into a beautiful purple and white room! Plaques with inspirational quotes were hanging on the walls, as well as photos taken on her weekly rendezvous with both Mr. and Mrs. Hamilton! There were also photos of her with her friends, and various clubs she was a member of.

The bed was way bigger than what she had at the orphanage, with Picasso themed bed sheets and pillows. At one corner of the room, there was an art section with an easel, table, rulers, pencils, and a seemingly endless collection of pastels, colored pencils, markers, and paints to choose from. There was a closet on the other side of the room that stretched across the entire length of the wall, until it reached another door which led to her own bathroom area.

She opened the closet doors and gasped at the amount of clothing, both folded and on hangers, shoes of varying styles and colors, and a wide array of accessories which included jewelry and scarves. The ceiling was a deep purple with millions of tiny white shimmering specks that imitated stars. She could not hold back her tears as she slowly spun around, absorbing the beauty of everything in the room.

She found the nearest chair which was at her desk, sat down, and started crying with her face buried in the palms of her hands. She somehow managed to say, "Thank you both so much." "It's alright honey," Mrs. Hamilton whispered while rubbing her back. Mr. Hamilton stepped out of the room to give the ladies a private moment. Elizabeth managed to calm herself down enough to properly say, "I am sorry."

"I am just so grateful for all of this. I feel blessed to have this family and everything that you all have done for me. I feel loved not just by the physical things I have received, but also from all that you both have done for me over the past year and more . I have been given an overwhelmingly great number of blessings in so many ways, but I don't have anything to give back. I wish I did but I don't, and that is so unfortunate because I don't want you to think I am ungrateful."

"Hey," said a voice from behind her. Mr. Hamilton entered the room, placed his hand on Elizabeth's shoulder, and said, "You don't ever have to give us anything in return for all of this at all. We love you because you are a great person with a beautiful soul. You deserve so many good things in this world; things that we can offer. You have blessed us just by being yourself, and we want you to continue to be yourself. We don't need anything in return."

"Just continue being who you are, as we help to mold and shape you into who you are meant to be." "Thank you," Elizabeth replied with a tear-stained face, and hugged both Mr. and Mrs. Hamilton. Moments later, Mr. Hamilton said, "We will leave you to settle in. Your mom-" at this, he paused and looked at his wife to see her reaction. She was smiling. "Your mom," he continued, "and I are going to get dinner ready, and maybe tomorrow you can get a full tour of the house and we can all talk some more."

"Does that sound good?" Elizabeth shook her head and said, "Sounds good." Mr. And Mrs. Hamilton then left the room. Elizabeth got up from the chair, and sat on her new bed. As she closed her eyes, she allowed herself to fall backwards onto the mattress. "Thank you God, for turning around my circumstances into something so beautiful. Mom and dad, I love you both. I know you will always be watching over me."

"May I never forget to be grateful, and may I never forget the love I received from you both." With this, Elizabeth breathed a satisfied sigh and smiled to herself.

112

***

Chapter Nineteen

Family Name

Sam was lost in thought but said after a few minutes, "Do you think she is going to be okay? Everything has been going so well for her up to this point, but she hasn't heard back from any colleges yet. I am so scared for her David. Do you think she will get into MIT? I mean her grades are remarkable!" "Don't worry honey, she will be okay. It is still too early for her to get a response from any colleges. Relax, she will be alright."

"She has us," David said as he took the shrimp out of the freezer for dinner. Samantha glimpsed Elizabeth standing at the entrance to the kitchen shyly. "You can come honey," she said and Elizabeth shyly entered the kitchen, and sat down on one of the bar stools. "How are you feeling Lizzie?" Sam looked at her husband, quite surprised at his greeting, "I'm sorry," he said as he saw the expression on Sam's face.

"Is it too soon?" Elizabeth smiled and replied, "No I like it actually. I need to ask you guys something. Two things actually. The first is this. Will I be able to call you both mom and dad?" Sam and David looked at each other and smiled. Sam placed her hand on Elizabeth's on the counter and replied, "Of course you can." Elizabeth smiled and said, "Okay great. That is one question. My other question is this."

"I don't know how this works but my family name is Adams as you both may already know. I no longer have any family members remaining as far as I know. My current name reminds me of a family that is long gone. A family name is important to me and I am not asking this because I want to be a different person or anything like that at all. I will never forget my parents, or the love I have for them. Just like I know you will never forget your daughter."

"You both are my family now and I am on this journey with you, that is why this part is important to me. So with your permission, can my name be changed to Elizabeth Adams-Hamilton? I am blessed enough to have two families and this name reminds me of that." Elizabeth stared down at the counter, fearing that the answer might be in the negative. After a few seconds of silence, she heard Mrs. Hamilton say, "We will love that if you really want to. We wouldn't mind at all."

"I can get the paperwork done as soon as possible, so are you sure?" David asked. "I'm sure," Elizabeth said, as she looked up from the counter and smiled at them.

Chapter Twenty

Plans

"So, what are you going to do now with the orphanage?" David asked Sam, as she was snuggled with him on the sofa watching game shows. "Actually, Melissa will be taking over until I return to work. She has been training under me as my assistant for years, so I know she will do great. She has proven her efficiency time and again, so I have much faith in her performance. Who knows how long she will have to hold the position."

"Maybe until Liz starts college, or until you retire," she said in a sarcastic tone. With this, David chuckled and replied,

"Fair enough." "Melissa will be keeping me posted daily though, and I will be in communication with her every night to get the full events of the day, as well as to lend my guidance accordingly. I will be in office only if I need to be, but Melissa will handle everything else with the team."

"There is so much I want us to do as a family, and so much I want to teach Liz. We just got her and she will be going to college soon," Sam said disappointedly. David tried to comfort her by rubbing her shoulder. He then said, "Don't worry, you will still have me." "Not really. You will be working," she said. "I have not claimed my vacation time for years. It was brought to my attention and I decided that I really should seize the opportunity."

"We can get our daughter settled, and we can have time for ourselves," David replied, pleased that he pleasantly surprised Sam. Sam gently touched her husband's face, and playfully hit his cheek before asking, "When were you going to tell me?" He laughed and replied, "Now is as good a time as any." David suddenly got an idea and told it to Sam. "We all got the closure we needed didn't we? We found out about what really happened that day with the accident, and about the ones we lost."

"We love our daughter and Liz loves her parents. Why don't we go to the beach this Sunday, light a lantern in their memory, and let it drift off into the sky? It will be a beautiful moment for all of us. We all lost beautiful people that mattered to us, but we are all one beautiful family now," he suggested. "I think it is a great idea honey! We can tell Liz tomorrow and see what she says," Samantha replied quite pleased with the idea.

"When does your vacation start?" she asked. "It started today," David confessed to her smiling, while she stared at him in shock. "For three months," he continued. "David Hamilton, I can't believe you," she said, removing herself from his embrace. "You say that, but I can see from your eyes that you are happy," he said, as he moved closer to her. "I am, but I'm still mad that you didn't say anything. You really are in the business of surprises aren't you?" she stated as she playfully touched his chin and kissed him.

As Elizabeth lay in her bed that night, she rolled onto her side, and removed the photo from her bedside table; the photo she loved so much of her parents. "Thank you for always being there for me, even after you both couldn't physically be. Thank you for allowing this family to take care of me," she said. She then kissed the photo, and for the first time in years, she fell fast asleep.

Chapter   Twenty - One

***

Nadine's Conversation

"Good morning sleepy-head. Wow, you've showered and dressed already? Are we going somewhere?" David asked Elizabeth as she walked into the kitchen. "Good morning," she replied, feeling a little embarrassed. "Sorry, it has become a habit for me to brush my teeth and shower before officially starting my day." "That's a good habit honey, don't listen to your dad," Sam said as she gently hit David with the newspaper.

"Oh honey, I have an idea. Tomorrow evening, we can go to the beach and light lanterns." Elizabeth looked confused at David's suggestion. Even Sam had a confused expression, despite already knowing the idea. David then explained, "We all loved and lost someone that ironically played a role in all of us coming together as a family presently. We light the lanterns to honor their memory, and it floats away in the sky, seemingly becoming one of the stars."

"That way, we can always know that they are up there watching over us, as well as in our hearts." "I will love that! It sounds like a really awesome idea," Elizabeth said smiling. "By the way, your grandmother is coming over. She said she wants to speak with you. Don't be scared or shy. She loves you, and I am sure she just wants to tell you goodbye privately," Sam said as she stared compassionately at a very nervous Elizabeth.

"Ok," Elizabeth said trying not to sound nervous. Sam was perusing through some of Elizabeth's sketches in her room with her, when Nadine arrived. Elizabeth's blood ran cold as she didn't know the nature of the conversation she was about to have. "Come honey, let's go see mom," Sam said as she stood up and put out her hand for Elizabeth. Nadine sat in the formal guest room awaiting the arrival of Elizabeth.

Suddenly, a very shy Elizabeth joined her. Nadine smiled at the child and said, "No need to be nervous child, you are not in trouble. Come, have a seat next to me." Elizabeth, a lot less nervous at the smiling older lady, sat down next to her. "Now dear, my daughter lost her daughter years ago. David told me that it was the very crash that unfortunately killed your parents. I am so sorry to hear that."

"After the accident, Sam and David had been devoted to each other's recovery, and after that was accomplished, they devoted their time to work. There was always a void to be filled, and when she first called and told me about you, I knew that you both needed each other. My daughter isn't the type of person to get attached unless she is really and truly drawn to a person. It would seem like God took the unfortunate circumstances of the loss both of you experienced, and turned it around to create something so beautiful."

"You are our family, don't ever feel like you are not. You are adopted, this is true, but that does not mean that you are inferior. You have brought joy to Sam, David, and myself because of your kind demeanor and your vibrant personality. You are shy but I heard that you are no longer like this. I know it happens a lot now because you are in a different environment with different people, and that makes you nervous because you don't know what to do or how to act or behave."

"This feeling will pass with time. My granddaughter brought so much joy to me. She is gone now but her memory will never be forgotten. However, I have been granted a new granddaughter who brings joy to me even in her silence. God never makes mistakes dear. You are talented, and everyone has been placed on earth with a purpose. Discover that purpose and you will be unstoppable. You have a family now that loves and supports you."

"May you always know that you are loved. I leave for Rome tomorrow morning but I wanted to see you and speak with you concerning this before leaving. We all love you dear, never forget this. After these words, Elizabeth tightly hugged Nadine. After what seemed like the longest hug ever, Elizabeth let go. Nadine gently touched the girl's face and said, "I have to go but when I get back, we will have more to talk about and so much to do."

They smiled at each other as Elizabeth nodded in agreement. Nadine stood, smiled, and quickly went into the kitchen to say her farewell to Samantha and David. Elizabeth looked through the window of the room as she heard a vehicle pull up outside. Out of the car stepped Stephan! Before she knew what she was doing, she ran out the front door and straight into Stephan's arms.

"Wow, if I knew you missed me this much, I would've been here sooner," he joked. "I had no idea I missed you this much either," Elizabeth responded as she kept hugging Stephan. "I feel so loved," Stephan said before kissing his girlfriend. Their kiss was interrupted by Mrs. Hamilton's greeting. "Hi Stephan, nice to see you. Why don't you come inside? David is preparing sandwiches." At this time, Nadine was exiting the house to meet Sadie, who was just pulling into the driveway.

Elizabeth ran up to her and said, "Grandma, I want you to meet someone." She motioned for Stephan to join her. Nadine smiled at the presentation of such a handsome young man. "Grandma, this is my boyfriend Stephan," Elizabeth said. "It is a pleasure to meet you dear," Nadine said smiling. "Oh no, the pleasure is all mine," Stephan said as he smiled back at her. "Grandma is heading to Rome tomorrow," Elizabeth said.

"Is that so? Well I really do hope you enjoy it to the fullest, and hopefully I get the honor of talking about your trip with you when you get back," Stephan told her. "Of course dear. Such a handsome young man," Nadine said as she playfully pinched Stephan's cheek. "I will see you both when I return." "Of course grandma," Elizabeth said, and hugged her one last time before Sadie stepped out of the vehicle to help her in.

Sam, Stephan, and Elizabeth walked inside the house and headed into the kitchen. They were greeted with turkey sandwiches, carrot and celery sticks accompanied by dip, and drinks. "I came to tell you all something really important." With this confession from Stephan, David swallowed hard, as he thought maybe Stephan was here to propose to his daughter. The daughter he just got! "I got accepted into MIT!" he shouted.

Sam and Elizabeth gasped almost simultaneously. Elizabeth threw her arms around Stephan's neck as she congratulated him. Sam then gave him a congratulatory hug as well and so did David, which surprised everyone! He was just happy that Stephan didn't propose to his daughter, at least not yet. "Did you hear back from any colleges yet?" Stephan asked Elizabeth as he sat on the bar stool, and took a bite out of his turkey sandwich.

She sighed and replied, "Not yet, and it is nerve-wracking." "Don't worry, l believe that you will get in. You need to believe that too," Stephan consoled. "I do, but it doesn't take away the feeling that maybe I won't but enough of this nervous talk. Do you want to see my room?" Elizabeth offered. Sam and David looked at each other, their sandwich in mid-air between their plate and their mouth. "Sure, I bet it's pretty cool," Stephan replied as he got up from his chair.

"It is," Elizabeth said with excitement. Stephan started out of the kitchen. Elizabeth turned and whispered to her parents, "You have to trust that I am not going to do …you know…adult things." Her parents laughed, quite relieved at her assurance. She then turned, and led the way to her room. At this moment, Sam's phone rang. "Hi Samantha, its Melissa. Some letters came for Elizabeth at the orphanage and I was wondering if you would like me to drop by this evening and give them to you?"

"Thanks Melissa, that will be much appreciated. I'll see you this evening." Sam replied before hanging up the phone. "Anything wrong?" David asked, as Samantha slowly placed the phone on the countertop. She had a strange look on her face. "No, not at all," she replied. "Melissa is coming today to drop off some letters that arrived for Liz." "Do you think…." he began. "Yes," she responded, knowing his thoughts.

"I believe it is word from the colleges concerning her applications." "Why do you look so concerned? She is an outstanding girl. Any college would be happy to have her," David told his wife. "I know, but it doesn't take away the nervousness. I just want good things for her David. She has been through enough; seeing her family die, having friends taken from her, feeling alone because she thought no one wanted to adopt her."

"Despite all that, look at how far she has come. I just want good things for her," Samantha replied. David walked around the counter to where Samantha was sitting, laid his hand on her shoulders, looked her in the eyes, and said, "No matter what happens, whether she gets accepted to her college of choice or not, we will deal with it. God has placed her in our care to help her. The good in her life has outweighed the bad."

"Worse things could've happened to her but it didn't. She was kept safe for almost sixteen years so far, and she will continue to be safe. We will deal with whatever comes our way. No one ever wants to see their child hurt or disappointed. Good parents want good for their children but sometimes circumstances are inevitable. We will deal with it and move on knowing that nothing happens by chance." Words escaped Samantha at this point.

She just shook her head in agreement with his words and hugged him.

C h a p t e r   T w e n t y - T w o

✱✱✱

College Letters

As they lay on their back next to each other under the starry ceiling, Stephan took Elizabeth's hand in his. "We are both blessed, kind of like Job. Everything that was taken from us have been restored. I believe that we have to do good with what we have been given. I want to give back my talent to communities all over the world, helping as much as possible," Stephan said. "I want to do the same," Elizabeth responded.

"I think I have been blessed most of all," he continued, "with the most beautiful girlfriend ever. Even though you are so quiet, I know a lot about you already due to our years of friendship, and one day I will propose to you under the right circumstances. I don't want us to rush into anything but I do want to date you." At this, Elizabeth laughed and said, "I am already your girlfriend. Dating is when you are getting to know someone, to see if they are a suitable match for you permanently."

"But that doesn't mean that we shouldn't continue dating even afterwards. Not dinner all the time but just being in, and enjoying, each other's company. Hearing you laugh at the nonsense I say, and the corny jokes I make, is what makes me happy. Our journey through college is a new one. I know you haven't heard back from any colleges yet, but you will soon. A lot of relationships do not survive college but I would like to believe ours will, come what may."

"Or maybe you will find someone else more handsome than me-" Elizabeth turned sharply and stared at him when he made this remark. "Stephan, I need you to understand this. I am not your girlfriend just because you are handsome. You have a beautiful and charming personality, intelligence, morals, values, and a very caring heart, which is rare. It is actually very rare to possess all the qualities that you have, yet here you are with every single one of them."

"You have been by my side since the very beginning, helping me as best as you were able to. You had your own struggles, yet you didn't ask for anything at all in return. You have been a true friend, a worthy competitor where necessary, and a very honorable boyfriend. I wouldn't trade you for anyone or anything in this world. You have a beautiful soul, even with your corny jokes and awkwardness at times, but this is you, all of you."

"Nothing is hidden, and I love that because I love you." With this admittance, Stephan raised himself and kissed his girlfriend passionately. Elizabeth, quite taken by surprise at first, closed her eyes and kissed him back, quite absorbed in the moment. He then gently pulled away, looked her in her eyes, and said, "I love you too." Elizabeth smiled at him and said, "Since before your delightful gesture, we were talking about dating."

"Would you like to go on a date tomorrow with my family?" Stephan laughed and lay back flat on the ground as he thought about the proposition. "We are actually going to light lanterns and watch them drift away into the sky. The lanterns represent the loved ones we have lost. You have lost your parents, so I don't think my parents would mind you coming along as well." "That actually sounds like a great idea!"

"I would love to go with you guys. I think it will help me get closure. It sounds weird but it's true," Stephan replied. "I understand how you feel, trust me. It doesn't sound weird to me at all because I feel the same way," Elizabeth replied. "Now come, let us go downstairs before my parents think we are doing adult things." Stephan laughed and said, "You still say 'adult things'?" "Shut up," Elizabeth responded playfully. "Let's go".

While walking down the staircase, they were greeted by three nervous faces; David, Samantha and Melissa. Elizabeth slowed her walking, as her heart began to beat uncontrollably. "Is something wrong?" she managed to ask, as her slow walking no came to a complete stop. Her mother nervously stretched her hand to reveal five letters, each with the logos of their respective college clearly seen. Elizabeth felt a lump in her throat, but still managed to swallow.

She slowly stepped forward and took the letters from Samantha. David placed his hand on her shoulder and guided her to the living room, where she sat and stared at the letters before her. After what felt like forever, a voice pierced the silence. "We know you are afraid honey," Samantha said, "but whatever those letters say, we will deal with it accordingly, but we wouldn't know unless you open them."

Time seemed to slow down once more. Slowly, she opened all five envelopes and, closing her eyes, laid them all flat beside each other on the ottoman before her. She then opened her eyes and allowed it to rest on sentences throughout the letters; "Congratulations...", "We are pleased to inform you...", "You have been accepted...", "It would be an honor...", "We look forward to seeing you…".

Elizabeth's eyes widened with disbelief. Everyone gathered around her to read the words on the papers before her, and cheered with excitement with the contents of each letter. There was much hugging and tears of joy, even from Melissa who was so proud of the young lady she had come to know and love. Tears flowed from Elizabeth's eyes, and the excitement turned to silence as everyone looked at Elizabeth.

"Oh honey," Sam said as she sat next to her daughter. She felt helpless. In one swift move, Elizabeth wrapped her arms around her neck, and hugged her as her tears continued to flow. Everyone gathered around and hugged Elizabeth in one big group. "I am sorry that I am crying in such a happy moment," Elizabeth managed to say as she broke up the group hug. "I am just so grateful for all that has happened so far."

"I have a real family, true friends, and I feel so loved by all of you. Thank you very much for your love and support, and may I always be grateful for all that has been given to me."

Everyone gave her a grateful smile for the words she spoke. After a short pause, she shouted, "I choose MIT!" Everyone started to clap and cheer at her choice. David went into the kitchen quickly and reappeared with champagne and glasses.

"Let us toast this new beginning of a lifelong journey. We have a daughter, we have a great friend in Melissa who unhesitatingly assisted us throughout the past seventeen years, and we thank you Stephan for being a great friend and boyfriend to our daughter. You knew her before we did, and you have loved her with a love that is so evident, that I pray it lasts forever. Here's to what the future holds for us all."

With raised glasses, Sam exclaimed, "To a bright future for us all. May we be equipped to handle the road ahead. Cheers!" "Cheers!" Everyone responded unanimously as they all talked, laughed, and drank to the future.

Chapter Twenty-Three

*** ***

The Journey Begins

It was a beautiful starry Sunday evening at the beach. It felt like a solemn day for everyone because of the reason they were there, but nothing compared to the relief they felt in doing what was about to be done. Everyone wore white for the occasion; David and Stephan wore white three-quarter shorts and white linen shirts with the sleeves rolled up halfway. Samantha wore a white spaghetti strap maxi dress, and Elizabeth wore a white sneaker dress.

The boys got to work setting up the lanterns on the beach, while the girls went for a walk. "How do you feel?" Sam asked Elizabeth who looked deep in thought. "I am wondering what I did to deserve all that I have been given; a great family, the opportunity to study at a college of my choice, and a good boyfriend whom I wish becomes the man I am to marry someday." Sam smiled and confessed, "Sometimes, I wonder what we did to deserve you."

"Everything happens for a reason, and you remind me so much of my little girl and how I thought she would've turned out. God never gives us more than we can bear. She brought so much joy to us while she was here on this earth, and left a void that felt like a hole beyond repair when she was gone. We didn't choose you to replace our daughter, just like we are not here to replace your parents, but we are a family now."

"You are a super talented person with an unfortunate past, but we are here now to help you. We love each other, we will learn together, and we will grow together." "Thank you mom," Elizabeth replied. "What you just said means a lot. I feel guilty when I am enjoying the time together with you and dad because I sometimes forget about my biological parents, so I try not to be too happy so that I wouldn't forget them."

"Oh honey," Sam said as she stopped to look the girl in her eyes. "You don't need to feel guilty when you are happy. We will never forget the ones we lost, but they will never want our happiness to be locked away forever. Our loved ones live on in our memory, and we get to move on, help others, and live our lives, not restrict our own happiness. I love my daughter. I miss her more than anyone can know, but I find peace in knowing that she is in a much better place."

"I will never forget her, but I also will not let the ones that I can help suffer because I choose not to move on. When we lose the ones we love, we grieve and we move on because life waits on no one. Everyone grieves for different lengths of time and that is fine, but they move on when it is time to do so. That doesn't mean that we have forgotten our loved ones, it means that they have inspired the good that we choose to do afterward."

"That makes a lot of sense now that I think about it. Thank you mom," Elizabeth said as she hugged Sam. "I am sorry that I have to go to college so soon. I have not had enough time to spend with you guys at all." "Don't worry, we are going to celebrate your birthday with you before you leave, and your father and I have arranged for us to travel when you have your different breaks throughout the year. Who knows, maybe Stephan can come along as well."

Elizabeth blushed when this was said. "You really like him don't you?" Sam asked. Elizabeth blushed even more, but shook her head in agreement and said, "I know I am young and I have my whole life ahead of me. I don't plan on giving up on my dreams or college or anything like that for the sake of our relationship. I would never want to be put in a situation like that, because I know what I would like to do in the future would be to the benefit of so many people."

"But I do want a future with him. I'm almost sixteen and I may sound stupid, but I believe that we are meant to have our happily ever after with each other." "You don't sound stupid at all honey. Look at your father and I. We have had our differences along with our share of unfortunate circumstances, but I can't imagine myself going through both good and bad times with anyone else. We have our happily ever after with each other."

With this, Elizabeth smiled as Sam smiled back at her. "Sam!" The two ladies spun around when they heard the sound of David's voice. "It seems like your dad is ready. Let's go remind those we loved and lost, that we will never forget them." They then turned around, and walked briskly back to the guys, who smiled as they approached. "Ready?" David asked as they arrived. They both shook their heads in agreement.

David and Sam shared one lantern, Stephan had one, and Elizabeth had another. They all lit the little candle on the inside of the lantern. Sam whispered her farewell to her daughter and father saying, "I miss you my little dove. I miss everything about you, especially your laugh. You will never be forgotten. Dad, I love you and miss you more than words can express. You will never be forgotten either. You both will forever have a place in my heart and memory for as long as I live. I love you both."

David closed his eyes, and quietly said his goodbye to Anastasia and his father-in-law. When he was finished, he smiled at Sam, who smiled back at him, and they gently pushed the lantern into the starry night. Stephan closed his eyes, said his own little farewell to his parents, and gently pushed his lantern into the sky. Elizabeth whispered, "Goodbye mom and dad. I will never forget you both no matter what happens or how old I get."

"Thank you for always watching over me, and may I continue to make you proud." She then kissed the lantern, and gently pushed it into the sky. They all watched as the lanterns drifted up into the sky, until they looked like specks against the night's blanket of darkness. David took a deep breath, released it and said, "I think our loved ones are happy. May their memory always live on in our hearts." He then took Sam's hand in his while she was still staring at the lanterns drifting away.

She was startled a little, but smiled at her husband and

whispered, "Let's go home. Our child is leaving for college soon and I want to spend as much time with her as possible." David smiled back at her. They then turned around and started walking to the car. David then turned back to see Stephan and Elizabeth still staring at the drifting lanterns while wrapped in each other's arms. "I think we can give them a few more minutes," he said.

Sam smiled and said, "I see you're starting to like him." "He's a good guy with a bright future. They're good for each other. You were right, they're a good pair and I can't wait to see what the future holds for them." Sam and David continued walking to the car under the blanket of the starry night. They were quite content and curious about what the future held for them and their new family.

Camille Jeffers is an author, though a fairly new one, that resides in Trinidad. This country forms part of the Twin Island Republic of Trinidad and Tobago. She is the seventh of nine children and has enjoyed reading books from a very young age.

She has worked as a babysitter, clerical assistant, assistant teacher, candy store clerk, and sales clerk before she settled in her current job as a Personal Assistant and part-time author.

When she isn't working, she spends her time at home making plans with friends that never happen, reading books, writing, binge-watching television series, or enjoying scenic views in order to balance and calm her mind, as well as to provide inspiration for writing.

You can connect with Camille on Facebook at facebook.com/camille.jeffers or via email at camillejeffers@gmail.com

A c k n o w l e d g e m e n t s

There are a few people, without whom this book would not have been possible.

I am grateful to God for the talent that I have been given. May I continue to use it wisely and for the purpose in which it was intended.

The Trinity Hills Publishing Team have worked tirelessly and with much patience to make this book into what it is today. Thank you to my Publisher Dr. Mark Daniel and his entire team, who worked long hours to make my dream a reality.

I would love to thank my family members for giving me the inspiration, courage, and encouragement I needed to create the foundation for this story.

I would like to thank my friends who encouraged me in different ways to take a leap of faith, to write, and to eventually get published. Each of them has supported me mentally and emotionally, especially when I had second thoughts. Without them cheering and supporting me, I don't know if I would've been able to complete this journey. Thank you all.